TEQUILA MOCKINGBIRD

MORGANA BEST

BEST
Cosy Books

Tequila Mockingbird
(Australian Amateur Sleuth, Book 6)

ISBN 9781922420749

This is a work of fiction. Any resemblance to any person, living or dead, is purely coincidental. The personal names have been invented by the author, and any likeness to the name of any person, living or dead, is purely coincidental. This book may contain references to specific commercial products, process or service by trade name, trademark, manufacturer, or otherwise, specific brand-name products and/or trade names of products, which are trademarks or registered trademarks and/or trade names, and these are property of their respective owners. Morgana Best or her associates, have no association with any specific commercial products, process, or service by trade name, trademark, manufacturer, or otherwise, specific brand-name products and / or trade names of products.

GLOSSARY

Some Australian spellings and expressions are entirely different from US spellings and expressions. Below are just a few examples. It would take an entire book to list all the differences. For example, people often think "How are you going?" (instead of "How are you doing?") is an error, but it's normal and correct for Aussies!

The author has used Australian spelling in this series. Here are a few examples: *Mum* instead of the US spelling *Mom*, *neighbour* instead of the US spelling *neighbor*, *realise* instead of the US spelling *realize*. It is *Ms*, *Mr* and *Mrs* in Australia, not *Ms.*, *Mr.* and *Mrs.*; *defence* not *defense; judgement* not *judgment; cosy* and not *cozy; 1930s* not *1930's*; *offence* not *offense*; *centre* not *center*; *towards* not *toward*; *jewellery* not *jewelry*; *favour* not *favor*; *mould* not *mold*; *two storey house* not *two story house*; *practise* (verb) not *practice* (verb); *odour* not *odor*; *smelt* not *smelled*; *travelling* not *traveling; liquorice* not *licorice; cheque not check; leant* not *leaned; have concussion* not *have a concussion; anti clockwise* not *counterclockwise; go to hospital* not *go to the hospital; sceptic* not *skeptic; aluminium* not *aluminum; learnt* not *learned*. We have *fancy dress* parties not *costume* parties. We don't say *gotten*. We say *car crash* (or *accident*) not *car wreck*. We say *a herb* not *an herb* as we pronounce the 'h.'

The above are just a few examples.

It's not just different words; Aussies sometimes use different expressions in sentence structure. We might *eat a curry* not *eat curry*. We might say *in the main street* not *on the main street*. Someone might be *going well* instead of *doing well*. We might say *without drawing breath* not *without drawing a breath*.

These are just some of the differences.

Please note that these are not mistakes or typos, but correct, normal Aussie spelling, terms, and syntax.

AUSTRALIAN SLANG AND TERMS

Benchtops - counter tops (kitchen)
Big Smoke - a city
Blighter - infuriating or good-for-nothing person
Blimey! - an expression of surprise
Bloke - a man (usually used in nice sense, "a good bloke")
Blue (noun) - an argument ("to have a blue")
Bluestone - copper sulphate (copper sulfate in US spelling)
Bluo - a blue laundry additive, an optical brightener
Boot (car) - trunk (car)
Bonnet (car) - hood (car)
Bore - a drilled water well
Budgie smugglers (variant: budgy smugglers) - named after the Aussie native bird, the budgerigar. A slang term for brief and tight-fitting men's swimwear
Bugger! - as an expression of surprise, not a swear word
Bugger - as in "the poor bugger" - refers to an unfortunate person (not a swear word)
Bunging it on - faking something, pretending
Bush telegraph - the grapevine, the way news spreads by word of mouth in the country
Car park - parking lot

Cark it - die

Chooks - chickens

Come good - turn out okay

Copper, cop - police officer

Coot - silly or annoying person

Cream bun - a sweet bread roll with copious amounts of cream, plus jam (= jelly in US) in the centre

Crook - 1. "Go crook (on someone)" - to berate them. 2. (someone is) crook - (someone is) ill. 3. Crook (noun) - a criminal

Demister (in car) - defroster

Drongo - an idiot

Dunny - an outhouse, a toilet, often ramshackle

Fair crack of the whip - a request to be fair, reasonable, just

Flannelette (fabric) - cotton, wool, or synthetic fabric, one side of which has a soft finish.

Flat out like a lizard drinking water - very busy

Galah - an idiot

Garbage - trash

G'day - Hello

Give a lift (to someone) - give a ride (to someone)

Goosebumps - goose pimples

Gumboots - rubber boots, wellingtons

Knickers - women's underwear

Laundry (referring to the room) - laundry room
Lamingtons - iconic Aussie cakes, square, sponge, chocolate-dipped, and coated with desiccated coconut. Some have a layer of cream and strawberry jam (= jelly in US) between the two halves.
Lift - elevator
Like a stunned mullet - very surprised
Mad as a cut snake - either insane or very angry
Mallee bull (as fit as, as mad as) - angry and/or fit, robust, super strong.
Miles - while Australians have kilometres these days, it is common to use expressions such as, "The road stretched for miles," "It was miles away."
Moleskins - woven heavy cotton fabric with suede-like finish, commonly used as working wear, or as town clothes
Mow (grass / lawn) - cut (grass / lawn)
Neenish tarts - Aussie tart. Pastry base. Filling is based on sweetened condensed milk mixture or mock cream. Some have layer of raspberry jam (jam = jelly in US). Topping is in two equal halves: icing (= frosting in US), usually chocolate on one side, and either lemon or pink or the other.

Pub - The pub at the south of a small town is often referred to as the 'bottom pub' and the pub at the north end of town, the 'top pub.' The size of a small town is often judged by the number of pubs - i.e. "It's a three pub town."
Red cattle dog - (variant: blue cattle dog usually known as a 'blue dog') - referring to the breed of Australian Cattle Dog. However, a 'red dog' is usually a red kelpie (another breed of dog)
Shoot through - leave
Shout (a drink) - to buy a drink for someone
Skull (a drink) - drink a whole drink without stopping
Stone the crows! - an expression of surprise
Takeaway (food) - Take Out (food)
Toilet - also refers to the room if it is separate from the bathroom
Torch - flashlight
Tuck in (to food) - to eat food hungrily
Ute /Utility - pickup truck
Vegemite - Australian food spread, thick, dark brown
Wardrobe - closet
Windscreen - windshield

Indigenous References

Bush tucker - food that occurs in the Australian bush

Koori - the original inhabitants/traditional custodians of the land of Australia in the part of NSW in which this book is set. *Murri* are the people just to the north. White European culture often uses the term, *Aboriginal people.*

CHAPTER 1

Cressida Upthorpe banged on my bedroom window, but with Little Tatterford experiencing a typical heavy frost, and the world both outside and inside my bedroom freezing, I refused to get out of bed.

"The English are invading," Cressida shouted, yet not even Sandy, my yellow Labrador, stirred from her sleep.

I pulled the covers over my head. "Tell the Prime Minister." I could maybe fight one or two English people if they were very small or perhaps drunk, but a bunch of them? That was out of the question.

"You promised you'd help," Cressida said, her

tone pleading. "You must help or else I will tell everyone your darkest secrets."

"I don't have any." Still, I knew it was hopeless so stepped over Sandy and staggered to the front door. The fire, of course, was out. Open fires usually did burn all night, but something was wrong with the way my chimney had been built, so I always woke up to a cold house.

I opened the door to see Cressida, resplendent in a delicate crimson nightgown lined with fur and red gumboots also lined with fur.

She pushed past me. "Sibyl, I have the Fifth Earl of Mockingbird and his rather charming escorts arriving today, and I need your help at the boarding house. I can't ask Mr Buttons because the Earl is an old friend of his and wants to surprise him."

"I thought nobody knew Mr Buttons was living here?"

Cressida shrugged. "I suppose that busybody journalist told him."

I hurried over to the fire and pushed aside the firescreen. I checked that there were no coals still alight, then put some small logs in the fireplace before pushing several firestarter cubes under them. I fetched a bottle of metho and sprinkled it on the fire, and then flicked in a match, jumping backwards as I did so.

"How on earth does a man become the Fifth Earl of Mockingbird?" I muttered to myself as the flames soared.

"You wait for the previous four Earls of Mockingbird to die, I expect."

"What's his real name?" I warmed myself in front of the fire. The shivering was only just starting to subside when Sandy ran in and licked my fingers. "I'll feed you in a second."

"Thank you," Cressida said, but I was too cold and tired to correct her. "His name is Peregrine Winthrop-Montgomery-Rose-Bucklefort. He must be very posh, so I have to use the fancy silver."

I pulled a face. "And you said the Earl had an escort?"

"Yes, several. All up, it's a party of five. There's the Earl, his secretary, Lavinia Berkshire, his driver, Tristan Clemonte, and two other people named Jemima Hardy and Thomasina Chadwick. Some sort of assistants, I believe. Goodness knows what they do."

"Wow," I replied. "The English *are* invading. Are any of them drunk? Or very small?"

"You'll know soon enough. You're helping me to book them in. Dress for the occasion, won't you? These are very refined, elegant people, and they will expect a polished presentation and wonderful manners."

Ten minutes later, I stood outside the boarding house trying not to pull out my wedgie. I was wearing jeans that had fitted ten years ago but not so much after that. That was because all of my posh clothes—not that I really owned posh clothes—were in the laundry basket, so I had to resort to jeans and a blazer. The blazer was from the eighties and looked tragic—shoulder pads, hot pink, shiny.

"This is the best you have ever looked," Cressida shrieked when she saw me. "The very best. Only put on some makeup, dear."

"I *did*," I replied, offended. I'd actually caked my face with foundation *and* blush. *Like some sort of loose woman,* as my mother would say. Then again, she thought every woman was loose, even the ones who wore cardigans buttoned up to their necks and had huge spectacles that made them look like some sort of kindly wizard.

"Beauty is in the eye of the beholder," Mum

had said. "And some beholders love kindly wizards."

I snapped out of my reverie when Cressida tugged on the hem of my blazer. "Pink. So close to red and yet so very far."

Cressida had changed out of her red outfit into another red outfit, this one a tulle gown. I wonder what the refined English people would think of a couple of mad Australians—one escaped from a ball, the other escaped from the eighties—but shook the thought from my head. For the most part, we were a nation of convicts. The English landed gentry probably thought these were the only clothes we were able to steal at such short notice.

"Remember. Be polite," Cressida hissed in my ear as the car hummed up the driveway.

The car itself was quite posh, a BMW of some description. I wasn't up on fancy car models, as much as I admired them. The windows were blacked out. Surely this wasn't a hire car?

A moment later, the car came to a screeching halt, and onto the gravel tumbled the Fifth Earl of Mockingbird. He was wearing rather too-tight leather pants, and his black shirt was open all the way to his navel. Overpowering plumes of sickly sweet men's cologne emanated from him, and his long hair was a mess. He scrambled across the gravel and offered Cressida his hand.

"Delighted," he said.

I bit the inside of my cheek to stop laughing. I knew he was not what Cressida was expecting.

"I was expecting Peregrine Winthrop-Montgomery-Rose-Bucklefort," Cressida said sternly. She did not shake his hand.

"I am he. My attendants are Lavinia, Jemima, Thomasina, and Tristan."

"It's Tommie," Thomasina said.

"It's a pleasure to meet you," Tristan said. He appeared to be the only normal one of the bunch. The others, even the Earl, looked like hung-over rock stars with smudged eyeliner and wild, almost gritty hair.

"Hi." I shook Tristan's hand. He looked like an Oxford professor. He wore a tweed jacket, and his hair was swoopier than the magpies that swooped pedestrians to protect their young during spring. He reminded me of Detective Roberts, although I figured he was much younger.

"Have you been hanging out with Bill and Ted?" Tristan asked. He eyed my blazer meaningfully.

Cressida chuckled. "Oh yes, Lord Farringdon tells me you're referencing a movie about time travel." She picked up the purring cat. "Do come inside for a spot of tea." She turned to me and added in a stage whisper, "The English like tea, and Albert is presently removing crusts from cucumber sandwiches."

"Lovely," Tristan said. I offered to help with the bags, but he politely declined.

Cressida instructed everybody to leave their luggage in the foyer and showed them into the sitting room. Albert, the not-French chef, had placed silver trays of hors d'oeuvres on the walnut parquetry low-table between two bulky Chesterfields, with a large Victorian mahogany grandfather chair at the head.

As the Earl took his seat in the grandfather chair, he clicked his tongue in disapproval. "A Victorian nine-piece drawing room setting should consist of a single chaise longue, a grandfather chair, a grandmother chair, and six drawing room chairs of the balloon-back variety. What's more, one would expect the upholstery to match."

Cressida appeared most affronted. "I'll have you know that I am an artist, and my furniture reflects my taste!"

about that here. We're far from the sea, and we're too far south for crocodiles."

Jemima breathed a sigh of relief.

I pushed on. "Here we just have deadly spiders and snakes."

"Spiders and snakes?" Jemima looked at Tommie, whose expression mimicked hers. They both looked terrified.

"The Taipan snake is considered the deadliest snake in the world, so of course it lives here. Only a handful of people have been bitten and lived. But snakes are not all. There's the funnel web spider. They're highly aggressive. Still, if you live in a city and can get treatment in time, you might live. No, the redback spider, which is everywhere, by the way"—I paused to gather my thoughts as Tommie sniffled—"is Australia's black widow. Highly venomous. And naturally, they love to live in or around houses. Historically, the redback spider is responsible for the majority of antivenom used. I wouldn't get bitten by one if I were you. Just make sure to shake out your shoes before you put them on, and turn over any rocks or anything outdoors carefully, as redbacks live under everything outside. They're not aggressive, though." I smiled with encouragement.

Lavinia burst into tears. Tommie hurried to help her to the overstuffed, ancient couch blocking the light from the bay window.

Jemima snorted rudely. "She has a delicate constitution."

I wondered if I could sneak back to my cottage without the English people noticing me, but I felt so bad for upsetting Lavinia that I decided to stick around. Of course, redback spiders don't attack people and only bite somebody who accidentally touches them. Maybe I should have said that? Oh well. Too late now.

Peregrine looked up from his tea cup. "What happened to Lavinia, the jolly old stick?"

"She realised she is in Australia," Tristan replied with a wink at me.

"It's enough to make anyone woozy," Peregrine replied. "Hello? You, girl? Yes, your marmalade is most distasteful."

Tristan handed me the mustard cruet. These people needed to get their eyes checked, I decided. I also decided to hide the yellow paint tin in the hallway. Just in case.

"Sibyl, will you get the door? Lord Farringdon tells me Mr Buttons is approaching." Cressida nodded to the door.

I was halfway to the door when Mr Buttons let himself into the room. He stood among the antiques. He was looking at the English guests, and he seemed confused, his mouth gaping open.

Peregrine's face broke into a wide smile. "Surprise, Nithy, old boy!"

Mr Buttons dropped his polishing cloth. "Peregrine Winthrop-Montgomery-Rose-Bucklefort!"

CHAPTER 2

Mr Buttons rounded on Cressida. "What is this indecorous man doing here?"

Cressida's hand flew to her throat. "I thought you'd be pleased to see him! When he called me to book the rooms, he swore me to secrecy. He said he wanted to surprise you."

Mr Buttons shot the Earl a dark look. "I am *certainly* surprised. What are you doing here?"

The Earl walked over and slapped Mr Buttons on the back. "Come on, old boy, you know you're happy to see me. Like she said, I wanted to surprise you."

Mr Buttons glowered at him. "She? I assume

you meant Cressida. Please conduct yourself with some measure of propriety."

The Earl took Mr Buttons by the arm and guided him over to the back window, where the sunlight fell in patterns through the faded lace curtains. The two men looked unearthly, surrounded as they were by little dust particles dancing in the air.

I couldn't quite hear what they were saying at first, but it was obvious they were having an argument. I did hear the word 'manuscript' uttered several times. Finally, Mr Buttons said loudly, "I told you, I am no longer in possession of the manuscript!"

He walked back over to us, followed closely by the Earl of Mockingbird. "Come on, old chap, we can talk about it later."

Cressida raised one eyebrow. I had spent plenty of time trying to raise one eyebrow like Cressida and had always failed. I wondered how she managed to do it. Maybe it was because her eyebrows had been shaved off and pencilled on thinly. Either that, or she had particularly good forehead muscles.

As I continued to ponder Cressida's eyebrows,

Mr Buttons said in a churlish tone, "I suspect the only reason this *man*"—he almost spat the word—"has come to Australia is to try to procure a manuscript from me, a manuscript I no longer have. I donated it to the British Library some years ago, before I came to Australia."

The Earl of Mockingbird made a strangled sound at the back of his throat. "Nobody would donate something so valuable to a library! You can't expect me to believe that."

My curiosity got the better of me. "What sort of manuscript is it?"

I addressed the question to Mr Buttons, but it was the Earl of Mockingbird who answered me. "It's an illustrated manuscript with illuminated and decorative calligraphy, with an abundance of gold leaf and ink as well as silver used in the illustrations. It's medieval, worth a small fortune."

"And you think I still have the manuscript, so you came to steal it from me." Mr Buttons said it as a statement, not a question.

The Earl raised his eyes skyward. "Steal it? No, I simply wanted to see it."

"Nobody would come all the way to Australia just to *see* a manuscript," Mr Buttons said. "I assume you have discovered that Adrian Addison recently visited me, and you somehow coerced him to tell you where I was, despite the fact I had sworn him to secrecy. You came here, thinking you could steal even more from me."

The Earl rolled his eyes. "My good chap, are you still banging on about that signed cricket bat you think I stole from you all those years ago? You simply misplaced it."

"How can one *possibly* misplace a cricket bat?" Mr Buttons asked, his tone churlish.

The Earl's face flushed a ghastly shade of red. "You're trying to change the subject. Can you at least show me the manuscript?" He spoke through clenched teeth.

Mr Buttons picked up the cleaning rag from the floor, dusted it off, and proceeded to scrub a small spot of dirt for the Earl's left shoe. After a small noise of satisfaction, he straightened up. "Must I repeat myself? I donated it to the British Library before I came to Australia. I gave up everything to come here and lead a simple life."

The Earl of Mockingbird crossed his arms over his chest. "Oh, come on now. No one really believes that, Nithy old boy."

"Do not have the audacity to address me by such an insufferable name," Mr Buttons said. "You are well aware I do not like being called that."

"How do you two know each other?" I asked.

"Oxford, of course," Mr Buttons said. "Although I look immeasurably younger than this chap, I can assure you we are the same age."

"I do believe you have given up all your wealth, so I thought you wouldn't mind giving me the manuscript." The Earl of Mockingbird's tone had changed from angry to pleading.

Mr Buttons threw both hands into the air. "Why don't you check with the British Library?"

The Earl looked quite put out. "When I questioned that journalist fellow, he did tell me you had donated it. I contacted the British Library, but they wouldn't tell me anything. They said if they did have it, it was probably in cataloguing and suggested I check back in a few years."

"I don't know what I can do. You've come to Australia for nothing." Mr Buttons pouted and then added, "Is that really the only reason you came all this way with your attendants?" He gestured to the others in the room. "It seems to be a consummate waste of time."

"Allow me to be the best judge of that." The Earl narrowed his eyes.

Lavinia walked over and patted the Earl's arm. "Now come and sit down. Don't get upset. Maybe you need a drink."

"Sure, I'll fix you a nice cup of tea," I said, but Jemima interrupted me.

"The Earl likes tequila."

"Do you have tequila?" Tristan asked Mr Buttons.

"It's over there, in the crystal Tantalus on the cedar chiffoniere." Mr Buttons offered a half wave.

Tristan patted him on the back. "Then fetch him one, won't you?"

I expected Mr Buttons to object, but after a dramatic sigh, he walked over to fetch the tequila. When he was halfway across the room, he turned. "Would anybody else like a drink?"

The Earl's attendants all said they would like tequila. Mr Buttons soon returned and handed everybody a glass of the golden liquid.

"I think I need something strong after that scene," Cressida said to me in a stage whisper.

We too took our seats in the sitting room. The light was dim, and I wanted to open the curtains, but Cressida always said the sunlight would fade her antiques.

The fake French chef returned. "I have zee hors d'oeuvres for zee all, *t'sais*?" he said. Cressida and I exchanged glances. I wondered why he kept up his pretence of being French after we had discovered he wasn't. He set down a tray in front of the Earl.

Lavinia and Jemima were arguing. Jemima snorted rudely and turned to Cressida. "That's an unusual painting." She gestured to a painting on the wall, featuring jockeys falling off horses in a steeplechase race, and the horses trampling the jockeys in the most bloodthirsty manner imaginable.

Cressida turned and beamed. "Yes, I named it, 'The Horses' Revenge.' I think it rather wonderful, if I do say so myself. It's some of my best work." She beamed widely.

Jemima crossed the room to peer at the painting. "Oh! I didn't realise up close that it's blood all over the ground."

"Yes, the horses have squashed the jockeys in revenge for making them jump so high and run so fast." Cressida nodded and smiled as she spoke.

Mr Buttons and I walked over too, ostensibly to look at the painting, although I kept my eyes averted and studied the ornate gold frame instead.

"Are you a professional artist?" Jemima asked her.

Cressida was clearly pleased. "Not exactly, as I run this boarding house, but I *do* sell my paintings for a considerable sum."

Mr Buttons made a strangled sound.

Cressida turned to him. "Did you say something?"

"Not at all. Not at all."

"Are all your paintings like this?" Jemima asked.

"Yes, they are!" Mr Buttons exclaimed in horror.

"Interesting," said Jemima. She pulled a look of distaste and then turned around, before emitting a bloodcurdling scream.

I too turned around, my attention at first caught by Lord Farringdon fleeing the room, his tail fluffed up like a toilet brush. It took me a moment or two to realise why Jemima had screamed.

The Earl of Mockingbird had fallen back in his chair, his tequila now splashed over the ground at his feet.

He was dead.

CHAPTER 3

Cressida pulled me aside. "Another murder! How can this be?"

I shook my head in disbelief. I wanted to look away from the scene before me, but I couldn't quite manage to do so. Slowly, something dawned on me. I grabbed Cressida's arm. "Murder? It could have been a heart attack. Maybe he had a medical condition."

I didn't voice what I was thinking. Had the tequila been poisoned?

I looked around the room. The others were standing there, staring at the Earl of Mockingbird. Everyone was speechless and appeared to be in shock.

I hadn't heard Mr Buttons move behind me. "You had better call Blake, Sibyl."

I shook my head to clear it and then pulled my mobile phone from my jeans pocket. Blake had only arrived back in town that morning, and we intended to catch up for dinner that night. I had last seen him when Cressida suggested I could buy the land on which my cottage stood, and Blake had suggested that maybe another person could buy it with me. That other person, of course, was him. We hadn't had a chance to speak further, because he had been called away to Sydney to give evidence in a trial. The trial had dragged on for ages.

"Hello," Blake said, but I cut him off.

"Blake, there's a dead person at the boarding house."

After a moment's hesitation, Blake said, "Not again!" followed by words that I had only heard previously from my cockatoo's beak.

I pushed on. "Yes, the victim was the Earl of Mockingbird." I thought that sounded strange, so I hurried to add, "Cressida has some new guests, all of them English, and one of them is the Earl of Mockingbird. Or rather, he *was*," I amended. "He's just now dropped dead with no warning."

Blake sighed deeply. "I'll be right there," he said before hanging up.

"The police are on their way," I informed everyone.

Tristan looked up, surprised. "Police? Shouldn't you call a coroner or whatever you have in your country?"

"It's likely he was murdered," Cressida said. "Or did he have a medical condition? Heart trouble?"

The English people looked blank and shook their heads. "Not that I know of," Lavinia finally said. "He hasn't been well lately, but nothing serious." Her hands flew to her cheeks. "Do you think he was murdered?"

Cressida nodded. "Yes, that's the way things are around here."

I elbowed her in the ribs. "We'll know as soon as the police arrive," I said, "but since you say he didn't have a medical condition, it's possible he was murdered. I'll have to ask everyone to come and stand over here by the door with me so we don't contaminate the evidence."

"Evidence," Jemima shrieked. "Evidence? You really *do* think he was murdered!"

"That's the logical conclusion." I took a deep

breath and let it out slowly. Surely not another murder in Little Tatterford?

Little Tatterford was a small country town in Australia. Murders rarely happened in such places, and it was exceptionally rare that a victim would be murdered by somebody who wasn't a close relative.

I remembered the time an infamous criminal had finally been caught after hiding out from the police in the bushland for months. Some people felt sorry for him because they said he had *only* murdered his cousin. Still, most of the English who had come to Australia had been convicts. Maybe that explained it.

"I've just thought of something terrible!" Mr Buttons said.

"More terrible than murder?" Cressida asked.

"Roberts and Henderson." Mr Buttons shook his head.

I groaned. Detective Roberts and Detective Henderson were absolutely horrible. I was sure Roberts had it in for the boarding house, and his manner left a lot to be desired. Henderson wasn't quite as bad, but that wasn't saying much. "Do you think they're still in town?" I asked.

"It's entirely possible." Mr Buttons pulled a

white linen handkerchief from his pocket and dabbed at his brow. "It is most unseemly. I have an urge to make everybody tea and cucumber sandwiches, but I don't think we should take our eyes off the suspects."

Lavinia swung around, her hands on her hips. "Suspects? How dare you call us suspects!" She jabbed her finger in Mr Buttons' direction. "You're the likely suspect. You and Peregrine were arguing just before he died, and you were the one who handed him the tequila."

Mr Buttons scowled at her. "Somebody had plenty of time to drop poison into his drink."

I cleared my throat. "Wait until the police get here. We don't know it *was* murder yet. And we certainly don't know the poison was in his tequila. Maybe someone injected him with insulin, a quick jab that he thought was a mosquito. Or maybe somebody placed a poisoned patch of a deadly nerve gas against his skin. Or maybe…"

Mr Buttons interrupted me. "I think that's enough for now, Sibyl. Why don't you keep an eye on the suspects, and I'll slip out to the front door to wait for the police?"

He left before Lavinia could say anything else. Cressida hurried to the door to shut it behind him. "I certainly don't want Lord Farringdon coming in and lapping up the poisoned tequila," she said, and after a glance at me, added, "Of course, the poison might not have been in the tequila."

The door opened, and Blake stepped through. He smiled when he saw me, and then his expression turned grim when he saw the body. "Detectives Roberts and Henderson are right behind me," he said. "I'll ask everyone to wait in the next room. I take it nobody has touched the scene?"

"No, we got everyone over here by the door as soon as we saw what happened," Cressida said.

Blake nodded. "The detectives will need to take your statements. I'll wait here for forensics to come and process the body." He gave my shoulder a little squeeze as I walked out the door and whispered, "I can't believe it's happened again! Be careful."

We filed into the dining room. I walked past the long table and opened the curtains. I didn't want to sit in gloom at the best of times and certainly not after somebody had been murdered. For once, Cressida didn't complain at the sunlight streaming into the room. Everyone took their seats at the oak table.

Albert Dubois, the chef, stuck his head around the door. "Strong tea with zee sugar for everybodee?"

Cressida nodded assent. "That would be good. Albert, make sure you don't take your eyes off the tea. It appears we have a poisoner on the loose."

A collective gasp went up from the guests. I expected Lavinia would protest again, but the door flung open, and there appeared the most unpleasant person of Detective Roberts.

"I was about to go back to the city, but I said to Henderson we might as well wait for the next murder at the boarding house," he spat. "And I suppose this time you'll tell me you had nothing to do with it." He glared at Cressida.

"Careful what you say, young man, or you'll be hearing from my lawyers," she countered.

Roberts ignored her and nodded to the door. "Henderson will question you first."

Cressida pursed her lips and left. Roberts flipped open his notepad and pulled a pen from his pocket. It seemed the pen did not want to work, so he muttered to himself while jabbing the pen on the paper. Finally, he seemed satisfied. "And the name of the victim?" He looked at the English guests.

Tristan was the one who answered. "The Fifth Earl of Mockingbird."

The detective's bottom lip jutted out. "That was his name?"

Tristan shook his head. "His title. His name was Peregrine Winthrop-Montgomery-Rose-Bucklefort."

"And when did he arrive at the boarding house?"

"This morning," Tristan supplied. "We all came with him."

The detective nodded without looking up from his notepad. "And the purpose of his visit?"

"He came here to see Lord Nithwell."

The detective looked up at Tristan. "Who?"

"Mr Buttons," I said.

The detective stepped forward. "Mr Buttons. I see. Did you know the victim?" His eyes danced with anticipation.

"We knew each other many years ago," Mr Buttons said. "Peregrine was a most unsavoury fellow. I'm afraid I cannot have a good word to say about him, deceased or otherwise."

"That's for sure, as you had a big argument with him right before he died," Lavinia said.

I rubbed my forehead. If only she had not said that! Maybe she was the murderer and was trying to throw Mr Buttons under the proverbial bus.

Roberts smirked from ear to ear. "Old enemies, were you?"

I expected Mr Buttons to deny it, but he said, "Yes, I suppose you could say that. We didn't have time for each other. I thought he was the most repugnant fellow. He came here demanding to see a rare manuscript which I had donated to the British Library many years ago. The nerve of the chap!"

"And that's what you were arguing over?" Roberts pressed.

"Certainly. He said he had come all the way from England hoping I would give him the manuscript due to the fact I had given up the rest of my wealth. He didn't want to hear that I had already donated it to the British Library."

"So, you could say that's a motive then," Robert said, altogether too smugly.

"Who was his heir?" I said to nobody in particular. "Who is the heir to the Earl's estate?"

The English guests looked at each other.

"We, um, I don't know," Lavinia said. "He didn't have any children or wives."

"So, who inherits his wealth?" I said.

Roberts rounded on me. "It is *I* who ask the questions, Ms Potts. Kindly allow me to do so." To Tristan, he said, "So, who inherits his wealth?"

Tristan shrugged. "There *was* no wealth. Well, not millions any more. Maybe one or two million." He looked downcast. "That's why he was so keen to come here and get the manuscript from Mr Buttons. Since Peregrine had heard Mr Buttons had given up all his wealth, he thought he wouldn't mind giving him the manuscript when he told him how broke he was, down to his last million or two."

Lavinia and Jemima both gasped. "He wasn't down to his last few millions," Jemima protested. "How could you say such a thing?"

Lavinia burst into hysterical sobs.

Tristan's face flushed. "I'm sorry, Jemima, and you too, Lavinia. Peregrine swore me to secrecy. He thought the two of you would think less of him if you knew he had lost the bulk of his wealth. He lost it gambling, you see, and he owed some rather nasty people a substantial sum of money. He was hoping to get the manuscript from Mr Buttons and sell it to pay off all his debts, to get those people off his back."

I shot a sideways glance at the detective and risked another question. "Isn't that a little tenuous?" I asked. "I mean, coming all the way from England on the off chance Mr Buttons would give him a highly valuable manuscript? Why would he think Mr Buttons would do such a thing?"

"Peregrine said Mr Buttons was too generous for his own good," Tristan said. "Detective, do you think Peregrine was murdered?"

Before Roberts could answer, Henderson barrelled into the room. "It was murder all right!" he exclaimed to all. To Roberts, he said, "You've got to see this!"

CHAPTER 4

Detective Roberts pointed to each one of us in turn. "Nobody is to leave this room." His face formed into an ugly scowl.

He charged through the door, slamming it behind him. Mr Buttons and I hurried to the door. I put my ear against it, and Mr Buttons looked through the keyhole.

I could make out a few words. After an interval, Mr Buttons nodded to me. We returned to our seats just as Roberts stuck his head around the door. He seemed satisfied, as he shut the door once more after shooting me a glare.

"Did he say methanol or ethanol?" Mr Buttons asked me.

"I'm pretty sure he said methanol."

Mr Buttons tut-tutted. "Then maybe he was poisoned with metho. Oh dear, how indecorous."

"What's metho?" Tristan asked me.

"I don't know what you call it in England, but metho is short for methylated spirits. In America, I think they call it denatured alcohol."

"But where would the murderer procure it?" Tristan asked.

I shrugged. "Metho is everywhere in Australia. We use it for cleaning windows, adding it to the water we clean floors with to make them dry faster, and I pour it over firewood and then flick a match onto it to start the fire quickly."

Mr Buttons shook his finger at me. "And that is most dangerous, Sibyl. I have asked you many a time not to do that."

"So somebody put methylated spirits in poor Peregrine's tequila?" Lavinia burst into a fresh bout of sobs.

I shook my head. "No, I doubt it. I was worried about using metho in my cottage and especially around my dog and my cockatoo, so I researched it to see if it was safe. I discovered that metho itself doesn't have much methanol in it. I doubt whether a big drink of metho would kill anybody."

"Then where would one procure methanol?" Mr Buttons asked. "And is it colourless and odourless? His tequila looked normal to me."

Now Jemima was sobbing, so I elbowed Mr Buttons. "Maybe we should discuss this later."

He caught my meaning. Before he could respond, Detective Roberts chose that moment to return. He insisted Mr Buttons accompany him for questioning, while Detective Henderson said he would question me.

Henderson took me to the far corner of the dining room, to two antique, over-stuffed chairs whose sturdy wooden legs showed the evidence of Lord Farringdon's claws over time.

Henderson sat with his back to the wall, no doubt so he could keep an eye on the others. He spoke in hushed tones. "Tell me everything you can remember, Ms Potts, no matter how insignificant it seems to you."

I told him everything I could remember in great detail. "And then the cat ran out of the room, and his tail was fluffed up like he had put his paw in an electric socket," I concluded.

Henderson seemed perplexed. "I fail to see how that is pertinent to the matter at hand."

"You told me to tell you everything I

remembered, no matter how insignificant," I countered.

"Are you playing with me, Ms Potts?"

I was exasperated. "I'm only trying to do my best."

Henderson frowned and then shrugged. "All right then, please continue."

"Well, that was it. It was only after Lord Farringdon ran out of the room that I saw the victim. He was clearly dead, and he had spilt his tequila on the floor."

"Was anyone with him?"

I shook my head. "No. We were all looking at Cressida's painting."

Henderson shuddered. "Ah yes, her paintings." He shuddered again. "*All* of you?"

I nodded. "Yes, that's right. I think so anyway."

Henderson seemed satisfied. "That's all for now, Ms Potts. You may leave the room. You are not to go anywhere near the sitting room because it's a crime scene. Do you understand?"

I nodded and stood, but he gestured I should sit down again.

"Do you have any idea how he died?"

I thought the question a strange one. "I

assume he was poisoned. After all, he was drinking tequila, and I didn't notice him eating anything."

The detective nodded. "That's all for now, but please make yourself available should we need to question you further."

I stood up. "Thanks." I left the room as fast as my legs could carry me without looking too keen to escape. I found Mr Buttons in the kitchen complaining to the chef.

"Mr Buttons!" I exclaimed. "I thought Roberts would give you a good grilling. Henderson has only just now finished with me."

"He *did* give me a rather good grilling, I'm afraid," Mr Buttons said. "That detective is the most insufferable man. I'm sure I am his prime suspect."

"But you didn't even know the Earl was coming," I protested. "I told Detective Henderson that, and I told him you were surprised to see the Earl of Mockingbird. You wouldn't have had time to plan anyone's murder."

"Detective Roberts thinks otherwise," Mr Buttons said. "I think perhaps I should procure the services of a lawyer."

"Surely not, Mr Buttons!" Albert stepped

forward, brandishing a wooden spoon. "Surely not," he repeated in his Australian voice. "Obviously, one of his attendants killed him, either the English women or English man. One of them did it, you mark my words. That cop will come to his senses sooner or later."

I leant across the table and patted Mr Buttons' hand. "Blake won't let him arrest you."

"Blake won't be able to help this time, I'm afraid, Sibyl. I'm certain Detective Roberts thinks I did it."

"But what possible motive could you have?" Albert asked.

"You don't need a motive in Australian law," Mr Buttons lamented.

"Yes, but they still need a case to arrest you," I pointed out. "Did he say why he suspects you?"

Mr Buttons sighed before sipping his English Breakfast tea from a Royal Worcester tea cup, hand painted with fruits and partly coated with gold. "I have a feeling in my bones, Sibyl. The detective said it was unlikely one of the companions murdered Peregrine because they already had plenty of time to do so. He said it seems to him a rather strange coincidence that Peregrine was murdered as soon as he set foot at the boarding house. He asked me if I was so angry to see an old enemy of mine that I grabbed the first poisonous substance I could find to put in his drink."

I was furious. "Then we need to have a good look around that room before that idiot detective goes in there and destroys all the evidence by stomping all over it with his oversized feet."

Mr Buttons brightened up. "Exactly, but the door is locked, and Roberts is questioning people in the adjoining room."

"Then we'll just have to go through the window," I said. "We will have to wait until they take the body away, of course."

"But we can't do that," Mr Buttons protested. "We need to get in there before the forensic team comes and bags everything."

"I suppose you're right. I know, we can take photos and videos with our phones."

Mr Buttons stood. "What a good idea, Sibyl. Now, let's slip out the back door from the kitchen and skirt around the outside of the building until we come to the sitting room. We will let ourselves in through that window and have a good snoop around."

I motioned for him to stop talking. "Did Roberts mention methanol to you?"

Mr Buttons shook his head. "No, he didn't, as a matter of fact. Did Detective Henderson mention it to you?"

"No, he didn't either. They're probably trying to keep that under wraps to see if anybody lets it slip."

"One of Peregrine's companions must have brought the methanol with them, because I'm certain we don't have any around here," Mr Buttons said. "I am certain the murderer poisoned Peregrine with methanol to throw suspicion onto me."

"Yes, the murderer wanted to frame you," I said thoughtfully. I tapped myself on the side of my head. "Of course! That explains the timing. Somebody murdered the Earl of Mockingbird just to make it look like you did it! The murderer wanted to frame you to throw suspicion off themselves."

"Precisely!" Mr Buttons exclaimed. "And it seems the murderer plotted my framing down to the last detail, and this is why I am afraid I will be arrested for the murder."

CHAPTER 5

Mr Buttons and I walked around the side of the building. I crawled on my hands and knees under some of the windows, much to Mr Buttons' discomfort. When I stood up, he pulled a white linen handkerchief from his pocket and dusted the grass from my knees.

I was dismayed to see the sitting room window was shut firmly. "Oh no! What on earth are we going to do? I thought this window was always open just a fraction and couldn't be shut properly."

"No, I think that's the dining hall window," Mr Buttons said. "Come on, Sibyl, we'll find something in the tool shed."

Mr Buttons strode eagerly to the tool shed. I was not so eager, as I was worried about the redback spiders in the shed. It was an old, corrugated iron shed with plenty of nooks and crannies, the very places where redback spiders like to live. Mr Buttons opened the door and gently lifted the lid off one of the toolboxes. He hauled out a screwdriver and a paint scraper.

"Will that work?" I asked him.

"We'll soon know." He pulled a packet of baby wipes from his pocket and wiped the tools thoroughly until they shone and then dropped the baby wipes in the rubbish bin. I knew better than to say anything.

We hurried back to the window. "What if we get caught?" I asked. "Is there anywhere to hide in there?"

"Let's just see if we can get inside first."

I tapped his shoulder. "Okay, but if we do get inside, let's find somewhere to hide before we look."

Mr Buttons nodded. "Agreed."

He managed to open the window with the screwdriver, but it wouldn't open more than a tiny gap. He shoved it to no avail. Finally, he said, "Brute strength will not help, as I feared."

He stabbed at the edges of the window several times with the screwdriver and jiggled it this way and that. Finally, it squeaked open a little. "I don't know if I can squeeze through there," he said.

"That's okay, help me through it, and I'll go in alone."

Mr Buttons looked affronted. "I wouldn't hear of such a thing, Sibyl. There's plenty of room for me."

I looked at the gap and looked at Mr Buttons' rather rotund figure. "Well, if you're sure."

"You can push me if I get stuck."

My stomach sank. I had a feeling this wasn't going to turn out well. "If you insist."

I made a stirrup with my hands to give Mr Buttons a boost, but he had already nimbly raised himself to the window, and his head and shoulders had disappeared from view. I had forgotten for a moment he had been a prize-winning gymnast back in the day. He shimmied forward until he got stuck. Well, that was inevitable.

"Quick, push me, Sibyl!" came the muffled cry.

"Why don't I pull you out? I think you're

stuck. If I push you any further, you'll get stuck harder."

"Poppycock! Be a brick, Sibyl, and push me harder, and I'll be through the window in a jiffy, you'll see."

I rolled my eyes. I thought of the detectives discovering Mr Buttons wedged in the window. Whatever would they think? Still, he had insisted, so I grabbed his feet and pushed with all my might.

After a few minutes, he hadn't budged so much as an atom, of that I was certain.

"Good grief, I'm stuck," Mr Buttons said after an interval, stating the obvious.

"You think?" I muttered. In a louder voice, I said, "Can you get back out?"

"See if you can get the window up a little more."

The screwdriver was lying on the ground. I picked it up and moved it around the edges of the window. I put my shoulder under the window and pushed up with all my might. It moved a little.

"I think that helped," Mr Buttons said. "Quick, before the police come. Push me."

I lifted up his legs and pushed. He himself was

wriggling, and that seemed to move him a little further.

Without warning, my cockatoo appeared and landed on my shoulder. "Max, what are you doing here?" I exclaimed. "You go straight back home."

Of course, I knew Max wasn't a dog and wouldn't listen to me, but it was the first thing that came into my head.

Max took a look at Mr Buttons stuck in the window. "Look at that big fat bottom," he squawked.

"What did you say, Sibyl?" Mr Buttons said.

I stuck my head close to the window. "It's Max! He flew out of the window when Cressida came this morning. I haven't seen him since, and he just turned up."

"Never mind that now, Sibyl. The police could be here at any minute, and we can't let them find me here. Do something!"

"You're a silly old fool," Max squawked. "&^*%$ you!" He flew onto the back of Mr Buttons' leg and stuck his beak into poor Mr Buttons' bottom. Mr Buttons let out a loud shriek and at once disappeared through the window.

My first instinct was to turn around and run, but I resisted the urge. Max flew away, obscenities coming out of his beak one after the other. I stuck my head through the window to see Mr Buttons sitting on the floor. His mouth was wide open, forming a perfect O, and both his hands were clutching his cheeks. His eyes were glazed over. I squeezed through the window as fast as I could, spurred on by the thought Max might fly back and peck me on my bottom too.

I landed heavily beside Mr Buttons. "Are you all right?"

Mr Buttons took a while to speak. Finally, he said, "No, I am not all right. Your pest of the feathered variety has taken it upon himself to peck my derrière. It hurt, I can assure you."

I patted Mr Buttons' shoulder. "I'm terribly sorry about that. Still, we have to hurry. We can't let the police find us. Let's look for a hiding place first before we snoop around the room."

Mr Buttons continued to sit there staring blankly, so I took it upon myself to look for a good hiding place. A Victorian mahogany chaise longue sat at the back of the room. There was plenty of room under it, so I grabbed the throw rugs that had been placed over it for Lord Farringdon and lowered them until they touched the floor. I placed cushions on top to hold them in place.

There were plenty of Japanese Peace Lilies and Golden Cane Palms in the room, and I wasted no time moving them to the side and to the front of the chaise.

If somebody walked into the room and didn't actually search the room, we would be safe hiding there.

I walked back to Mr Buttons to point this out. He stood up. "Yes, that does seem to be a good idea. I don't think we could fit into any of the cabinets, so this will have to do."

I agreed. "It's nicely at the back of the room, so the police shouldn't have any cause to come over here. Anyway, if we're quick, we should be able to get out of here before they arrive."

It occurred to me that Mr Buttons would not be able to climb back out the window, given that he'd had so much trouble getting in. Still, we would have to cross that bridge when we came to it. For now, we had to snoop.

Mr Buttons handed me a pair of disposable gloves. "Put these on, Sibyl. I know our prints would be all over this room anyway, but we certainly don't want them on the victim or on anything he touched."

I pulled my phone out of my pocket and walked in front of the victim, trying not to look too closely at him. I filmed the area around him and the spilt tequila on the floor. I then walked back and took a video of the crystal decanters in the Tantalus, along with the brandy and all the other bottles of spirits and liqueur. The tequila bottle was missing. I assumed the police had taken it for analysis.

"Oh, my goodness me," Mr Buttons said.

I was at his side in an instant. "What is it?"

He pointed to a bottle on the small parquetry table. "That wasn't there before."

I bent over to stare at the bottle. It was small and black, with a red and white label. I took a close photo of it, and then peered to read aloud, "Methanol 99% Laboratory Grade One."

"That's bizarre," I added. "It even has the word 'methanol' on it."

Mr Buttons readily agreed. "Yes, it seems as though somebody was indeed trying to frame me. Why else would they leave a poisoned bottle so readily labelled like this?"

"Then the detectives have left it here for a particular reason," I said.

"Maybe to keep it safe in a locked room while they question everybody."

That seemed like a reasonable suggestion to me. "I took a photo of the label. We'll have to find out where this was sold." I thought I heard a noise outside the door so grabbed Mr Buttons' arm. "Mr Buttons, we need to get out of here right now! It might take you longer to climb back through that window. I mean, you could hide behind the chaise until the body goes and the police leave." I tapped my chin. "They've obviously searched in here already. As soon as they go, I can unlock the door and get you out."

Mr Buttons shook his head. "I would rather try the window," he said over his shoulder as he headed for the wall.

I followed him, protesting. "You were hardly able to get through the window, and I don't want you to get stuck. What are we going to do?"

"Sibyl, try the window and see if you can open it a little more," he said. "It should be easier from this side, considering the flooring here is raised much higher than the outside ground level."

I hurried to the window. I wedged my shoulder under it and pushed it as hard as I could. "I can't make it budge," I lamented. "If only we had some oil or something to make it slide."

"I don't think that would help it," Mr Buttons said. "These are old sash windows. In fact, if you push too hard, they might break. I don't know what to do. Sibyl, save yourself!"

"No way," I said. "If those detectives catch you by yourself, they'll think you did it for sure, but if they find us together, they'll simply think we were both snooping around the scene."

"Or maybe they'll think we were in it together," Mr Buttons pointed out.

Just then, we heard a sound at the door. "It's the cops!" I whispered. We both ducked down behind the chaise.

I was glad I had moved some of the Japanese Peace Lilies and the Golden Cane Palms to the side of the chaise, as they enabled me to peek out. To my dismay, it wasn't Blake but Detective Roberts along with Detective Henderson. "We'll have to question the suspects again later," Roberts said to Henderson. "We'll take them all down to the station for questioning, and hopefully that will intimidate them."

"It's strange that bottle of methanol was left out for us to find," Henderson said. "The perpetrator left it with the tequila and the other spirits." He gestured in my direction.

I ducked back and couldn't hear what Roberts said in response. Both men had been standing close together, looking at the bottle of methanol.

"They're a bit slow in coming to pick up the exhibit," Roberts said.

For a minute, I thought he was referring to Cressida's painting, but then I remembered that the police called murder victims 'exhibits.'

Detective Roberts pushed on. "We can't leave until they do come and collect it, because I don't trust those English people, and I certainly don't trust Mr Buttons."

I shot a look at Mr Buttons who was crouching down next to me. He simply narrowed his eyes.

I caught my breath as something brushed the top of my head. I thought it was a spider and bit back a scream, but then I heard Max's squawk.

"Run for the hills! It's the cops, it's the cops!" he squawked. I looked through a Japanese Peace Lily to see he was perched on the chair behind the victim.

Detective Roberts swiped at Max with his notepad.

"It's that dreadful parrot of that foolish girl's, Roberts," Henderson said. "She taught him to say obscenities."

Mr Buttons put his hand over my mouth. I nodded to him that I wasn't going to say anything. Still, I was furious. It was my ex-husband who had taught my cockatoo to say obscenities, simply to upset me. And, of course, it had worked. How dare that detective assume *I* was the one who had taught the cockatoo to say rude words? And call me foolish?

Detective Roberts swiped at Max again, and dislodged him from the chair.

"You're a silly old ^&%, Bobbits!" Max squawked. "Bobbits, you're ugly. Bobbits, you're a fool."

I saw Henderson doing his best not to chuckle.

"How did he get in here?" Roberts screeched.

Henderson pointed to the window. "That window's open."

"Was it open before?" Roberts demanded.

"I don't know. I didn't notice it, but I think the curtains were across it. It's windy outside, so maybe the curtains have blown open."

"That won't do it all. There's no point having the door locked if the windows are open, is there Henderson?" Roberts said in a lecturing tone. "Go and shut them at once."

Mr Buttons and I exchanged glances. We were about to be caught!

My heart was beating out of my chest. I tried to slow my breathing, but that only served to make me gasp for air. I had visions of being on trial for the murder of somebody I had only met that day.

Henderson had only taken a couple of steps towards us when Roberts shrieked. I turned my attention from Henderson back to Roberts and saw Max sitting on his head. Sulphur crested cockatoos are rather large birds and have sharp claws. I figured he was digging his claws into Roberts' head.

"Get it off me! Get it off me!" Roberts said as he spun in circles, flailing his arms.

"Spin, Bobbits, spin!" said Max.

"You're only alarming the bird," Henderson said. "You upset him by trying to hit him with your notepad. If you're calm, the bird will be calm."

Roberts called Henderson a few words that

made my cockatoo's language pale into insignificance.

The door opened, and some men covered in white clothing walked in with a trolley. Max at once flew out of the window.

Roberts recovered his composure pretty quickly, I had to give him that. "There's the body," he said, somewhat unnecessarily. Okay, maybe he hadn't recovered his composure too well.

With that, he stormed out of the room, with Henderson hard on his heels. It didn't take long for the men to wheel the body out of the room. The second they vanished from sight, Mr Buttons pulled me to my feet. "Come on, Sibyl. Our only hope is to go out that door."

We hurried over to the door, and to my relief, it wasn't locked.

I gingerly opened the door a crack and saw the backs of the men wheeling the body away on the trolley and the detectives following them.

Mr Buttons and I tiptoed through the door and hurried in the other direction. We hadn't gone far when Roberts' booming voice bellowed down the hallway towards us.

"Not so fast, you two!"

CHAPTER 6

"What were you doing, snooping around these hallways and corridors?" Detective Roberts demanded. "Were you listening in to police business?"

"Mr Buttons lives here," I said haughtily. "We were going outside for some fresh air, but when we saw the body, I was upset, so I asked Mr Buttons to go back to the kitchen with me."

"That doesn't explain why you were sneaking." Suspicion flooded Roberts' face.

I thought quickly. "If you must know, we didn't want you to see us," I said. "It's bad enough seeing the body of a murder victim, without being questioned by the police."

I was expecting Roberts to say that we

shouldn't worry if we had nothing to hide, but to my relief, he simply grunted and trudged back to Henderson. The two of them put their heads together and whispered, glancing at intervals in our direction.

"Come on, Sibyl." Mr Buttons pulled me back down the corridor in the direction of the kitchen.

I shut the kitchen door behind me and then opened it to peek out, but the detectives hadn't followed us.

"What is zee matter?" Albert asked in his fake French accent.

"It's those detectives, by Jove," Mr Buttons said. He took a packet of baby wipes from his pocket and wiped his chair, before discarding the baby wipe in the rubbish bin. As he took his seat, he added, "And my dear fellow, why are you speaking in that accent? Both Sibyl and I know you are not French, and there's nobody else here."

Albert waved a saucepan at us. "I have to stay in zee character, *mais non*!"

Curiosity got the better of me. "Why?"

"Because everybody knows that French chefs are the best, and the guests won't question my cooking if they think I'm French!" he exclaimed. "Social proof and all that!"

I was pondering his words when Cressida sailed in. "Sibyl, Mr Buttons, I'm throwing a dinner party tonight for the guests. And Albert, make sure you keep the kitchen doors locked from now on. We don't want to give the murderer any more opportunities to use poison, especially not on us."

I put my head in my hands. Cressida pushed on. "And serve asparagus. The English like asparagus. Isn't that so, Mr Buttons?"

I ignored the ensuing conversation about what the English *en masse* did and didn't like to eat. I didn't want to go to dinner. A man had just died, and Cressida wanted me to eat asparagus.

"Wear something devastating," Cressida told me as she bopped my nose with a powder puff hastily extracted from her handbag.

I sneezed. "Devastating?" I asked when I recovered. "I don't want to go to a dinner party, Cressida. I want to have some alone time with Blake. And besides, a man has just died."

She bent to pick up her cat and clutched him to her chest. "Exactly. Lord Farringdon said that tonight will be a good distraction as well as a chance to observe all possible murderers more closely. Meet me in the dining room at five sharp.

I'll invite Blake too, so you can both have some alone time with all of us."

I rolled my eyes.

Hours later, I returned to the boarding house. I found myself slipping behind the boarding house, desperate to delay any conversation with Cressida's English murderer guests.

"Sibyl?"

I was walking by the stone fence at the rear of the boarding house. The person silhouetted against the yellow light of the setting sun had called my name. It was Tristan. He was clutching a small glass.

"Whisky," he said, when he saw me looking at it.

"Are you okay?" I asked.

"It's been a bad day."

"You really don't need to go to dinner tonight," I said. "Cressida could have the food taken up to your room." Suddenly, I felt self-conscious about my attire. I had worn a red dress just to please Cressida, but the slinky dress felt a little too loud given what had happened earlier that day.

Tristan shrugged. "Have you seen the girls?"

I hadn't seen Jemima and Lavinia, no. But I

had seen Tommie. She had driven off at speed when I walked over from my cottage. I told Tristan as much, and he sighed.

"I never cared for the old fellow, you know. Terrible bore. But that doesn't mean I wanted him to be murdered." Tristan stared down at his drink. "I wonder how the girls are taking it?"

We both paused, and I heard the distinctive sound of Jemima and Lavinia fighting in the distance. "Did they like Peregrine too?"

"No one liked Peregrine," Tristan replied dryly. "And I expect that's why he's not attending dinner tonight." He skirted the side of the boarding house, and I followed.

The air in the boarding house was in sharp contrast to the cold, fresh air outside. I would never get used to the smell, dust, and ancient air, or the atmosphere, cold and haunting. I had no idea how Cressida could live here, but then I was more of a cottage girl myself. Give me a small house, a nice tea cup, and a garden full of flowers. That made me happy. Not a plethora of tightly packed antiques and creaky floorboards.

"There you are," Cressida said. "Wait in the sitting room, won't you, Tristan? The French chef will ring a bell for dinner." She pulled me into the dining room. "I saw you behind the house. Were you avoiding me? Having second thoughts about dinner, maybe?"

I didn't have time to speak before she shoved me into a chair at the dining table and handcuffed me to the arm. "What on earth?"

"You are not going anywhere," Cressida said. "I need your emotional support."

"And I need you to uncuff me."

'You're not going anywhere."

I scowled at her. "I'm not going anywhere now, no."

"Oh, there's the dinner bell. Sibyl, keep your hand beneath the table. I don't want my guests to believe this is a boarding house where we handcuff people to chairs."

"But this *is* a boarding house where we handcuff people to chairs, Cressida. Obviously!"

"Ah," Cressida said, ignoring me. "Here is Blake now."

Blake smiled at us as he stepped into the dining room. He was wearing jeans and a light jacket, his smile as boyish and gorgeous as always. I wanted to call out for help, but Cressida picked up a fork and glared at me. I was fairly certain she wouldn't actually stab me. I was also fairly certain that I could not take that chance.

Blake frowned when I didn't stand to kiss him on the cheek. "Is everything okay?"

"Poor Sibyl has seasickness," Cressida said.

"But, um, she's not on a boat!" Blake frowned even more.

"Just the thought of boats," I said weakly, "gets me all churned up. I had better sit for a minute longer. I saw one of Cressida's seascape paintings."

Blake nodded slowly. "Yes, that does explain it. Still, I'm not sure dinner here is a good idea," he said. "Why don't we go back to your house, and I'll make you some pancakes?"

Of course, I wanted nothing more than to flee this boarding house with the English possibly-murderer people and Cressida, to eat pancakes while Blake made me laugh until I snorted. But I couldn't abandon Cressida. Also, she had the keys to the handcuffs.

"Who is this scrummy man?" Lavinia burst into the dining room, passing Cressida on her way out. She was wearing nothing but a shirt and the briefest of shorts, and they were not really shorts but a handkerchief. A toy handkerchief you'd give to one of those ancient and horrendously scary porcelain dolls Cressida kept in the attic.

"Jemima, please put the bottle down," Lavinia added, as Jemima followed her into the room.

Jemima was wearing casual clothes. I kicked myself for overdressing. Or, looking at Lavinia, dressing at all.

"No!" Jemima slurred. She crumpled into a chair as Tristan poked his head around the door. "Is everything okay?"

"Yes, everything is fine," I said. "Tristan, this is my friend, Blake."

Blake's eyebrows shot skyward. "I'm her *boyfriend*, actually."

"Boyfriend," I said hurriedly. "Right."

"Charmed," Tristan replied. He quickly stepped into the room as Cressida swept by, wearing a ball gown and carrying a tray of champagne glasses.

"Friend?" Blake whispered in my ear.

"I didn't mean anything by it," I said, and I glanced down at my handcuffs in the hope that Blake would follow my gaze. But he was too busy fuming to notice his girlfriend had been shackled by a mad woman who ran a boarding house.

"I never liked him," Jemima sniffed, and she

took another swig of wine before throwing the bottle against the wall. It shattered, and the rest of the dinner party gasped. "He was a real prat."

Lavinia wiped away a tear. "He was lovely." She sniffled. "Thoughtful. Compassionate. Kind."

"Then why is he dead?" Tristan sneered.

"We're very serious, you know?" Blake said loudly.

Tristan appeared perplexed. "About what?"

"No," Blake replied. "Sibyl and I."

Tommie stormed into the room. "What's all this fuss about?"

This sent Lavinia into a fit of wails. "Tommie, how can you be so cruel. So, so cruel?"

Jemima sat to attention. "Stop with the act, Lavinia. You hated Peregrine."

"I loved him."

"I saw you two fighting the day before he was murdered."

"We had some passionate discussions from time to time," Lavinia said as she brushed away her tears. "That is not illegal."

"Murder is."

"Sibyl and I never have disagreeable discussions," Blake said pointedly to Tristan. "We agree on everything."

Tristan ignored him. "What was the fight about, Jemima?"

"How should I know? It seems so long ago."

Jemima snatched the champagne glass out of Tommie's hands. "Lavinia isn't the only one who had problems with Peregrine, was she, Tommie?"

"I didn't have problems with Peregrine," Lavinia sniffed.

Tommie crossed her arms. "What are you implying, Jemima?"

"Just that I saw you two fighting the day before he was murdered as well."

"That is not true."

"Yes, it is."

"Was anyone *not* fighting with Peregrine the day before he was murdered?" I asked.

No one spoke. I took a sip of champagne and eyed each guest meaningfully. No one made eye contact.

"Where is Mr Buttons?" Cressida asked all of a sudden, leaning forward and knocking aside the brioche toasts with ricotta and peas. "He should be here."

"He's taking a nap," Tommie said. "I happened across him earlier. The poor chap said he was dreadfully tired."

"I'm never tired," Blake said. "I have boundless energy. And I am spontaneous. Which Sibyl loves."

Everyone ignored him. The discussion turned to Peregrine's car, and I was able to whisper to Blake, "Why are you acting so weirdly tonight, Blake?"

"You called me a friend."

"You are my friend."

"Boyfriend, Sibyl. I'm your *boyfriend*."

I sighed. "I don't like Tristan."

"You could have fooled me."

"Hey!"

Blake's frown deepened. "And you're not acting your usual self. You've done nothing all through dinner but just sit there. No looking for clues. No searching for more clothes to wear."

"I'm handcuffed."

"Now is not the time for metaphors."

"No," I said, "I'm handcuffed to this chair. Cressida is refusing to let me escape this horrendous dinner party. Blake, there is nothing I'd like more than to eat pancakes with you right now and get away from these people."

Blake laughed. "I'll get the key. Don't worry about it."

But I didn't have time to reply to that. "Oh no! Jemima is hanging off the chandelier."

"I know. She's had a lot to drink."

"No. She is literally hanging off the chandelier."

Blake looked up. Jemima was cackling as she swung from the antique chandelier, while Lavinia tried to knock her down with a broom.

"Cressida," I hissed. I didn't need to ask her for the key—she knew this had gone too far.

"Fine." She uncuffed me just as Lavinia scored a direct hit on Jemima and knocked her onto the floor

"I'm going to kill you," Jemima hissed. She dove onto Lavinia and the pair collapsed onto the old tallowwood floorboards in a storm of shouting. Tristan managed to break them up while Tommie didn't make an effort to move. She looked at me, rolled her eyes, and shrugged.

I felt a hand on my back. It was Blake. "Let's get out of here," he said.

I didn't hesitate. We slipped out of the room in the chaos of Lavinia and Jemima fighting and walked in pleasant silence over to my cottage. My wrist still throbbed from where I had been handcuffed, and I made sure to pout and play up the pain so Blake would make a big fuss.

For the life of me, I couldn't understand why I had called him my friend instead of my boyfriend. Of course, I wasn't interested in Tristan, and of course, I was proud that Blake was my boyfriend. He was gorgeous, and he had a lovely personality. I always thought I'd have to pick one or the other. I was fine with that, being no supermodel myself, but boy was I glad that Blake had shoulders. Strong shoulders. And the face of a Greek god. Maybe not just any Greek god, but Apollo, a god of the sun. Yes. That was Blake. He bought the sun wherever he went, and I was so glad I was no longer in the dating game.

Dating was terrible. I had been on a million first dates that were a hundred times more terrible than tonight's dinner. That did not seem possible. Yet it was.

I clapped when Blake put a plate of pancakes in front of me on the table. So, with my dating life sorted, now all I needed to focus on was murder. I let Blake talk about sport while I ran through the clues I'd picked up at dinner. Well, two clues. Peregrine had fought with not one but two people in his party the day before his death.

So now I had a motive. Well, I would have a motive, once I had found out why they were fighting with him, and if it was a strong enough reason for one of the English guests to murder Peregrine Winthrop-Montgomery-Rose-Bucklefort, the Fifth Earl of Mockingbird.

CHAPTER 7

Tristan hurried over to me as I was slowly making my way to the boarding house, studying the gathering clouds and wondering if they would bring rain. "It's a disaster!" he exclaimed.

My heart raced. I caught my breath. "Has the murderer struck again?"

"No, but Cressida wants to me to go and buy tomatoes. I can't remember if she wanted red beefsteak tomatoes or green beefsteak tomatoes." He frowned deeply.

"Maybe you should buy Cressida both."

"Then she'll know I wasn't paying attention."

I chuckled.

Tristan pouted. "Cressida told me that she

refuses to serve anything less than the best, which means her chef needs the best ingredients—a task she has given to me."

"Well," I began thoughtfully, "why don't we look up what different tomatoes are used for? Let's see if we can't jog that memory of yours."

Soon I found myself huddled with Tristan over a phone, researching tomatoes. Red beefsteak tomatoes were apparently a big deal—quite literally. They were large and juicy and used in a base for dips. They could not be more different from green beefsteak tomatoes, which were used in things like artisan sandwiches. Artisan sandwiches did sound very Cressida, but the woman was also obsessed with the colour red. I didn't think she'd want to buy something as non-red as green tomatoes.

I scratched my head. "That's no help at all," I murmured.

"Come with me," Tristan pleaded. "Come with me and help me pick the right tomatoes. That way, Cressida can't be angry if we get the wrong ones or waste money on both."

I thought he was acting rather strangely. "Cressida never gets angry."

"Maybe if we get the wrong tomatoes, we could return them?" Tristan asked.

I shook my head. "No returns on vegetables."

"Are tomatoes fruits?"

"Let's check."

It turns out that botanically, tomatoes are fruits. However, in order to clarify customs regulations, the United States Supreme Court ruled that a tomato is a vegetable. That was no help, as we were in Australia. I wished I didn't know this much about tomatoes, and five minutes later, I wished I was not in a car with Tristan, speeding towards the fruit and vegetable shop.

Sadly, the shop had both kinds of tomatoes, so we couldn't even use the excuse of no stock. And if we lied to Cressida, she would know. She would take it as a personal affront, and I would never, ever hear the end of it. Eventually, Tristan and I decided on the red tomatoes. Yes, Cressida liked artisan food, but the woman loved red. That was the deciding factor in the end.

We walked back to the car, carrying the tomatoes like they were glass and set them carefully in the back seat of the car. I was somewhat irritated. I had better things to do than buy tomatoes. I supposed every person on earth had better things to do than buy tomatoes! If only Tristan had paid attention when Cressida first asked him to run down to the shops to buy tomatoes.

"She'll wonder where we are," Tristan said as I slid into the passenger seat. He wouldn't let me drive, which was a relief. I didn't want to be held responsible if the tomatoes turned into salsa on the way home thanks to some terrible driving. "Seatbelt on?"

"Yep," I said.

Tristan started the engine, and we headed for home. I didn't expect to see anything more than the occasional car. However, when we pulled out of town, a white ute started to drive very close behind us. I tried not to feel too worried. My father always panicked when someone tail-gaited his car, and to the best of my knowledge, he had never once been in an accident. So why did I need to worry?

"There's a car behind us. Isn't he a bit close?" Tristan said, glancing at the car in the rearview mirror. "Do Australians often drive like that?"

"Yes," I lied. I figured if Tristan panicked, then I would panic too.

Suddenly, the ute following us pulled out and

drew level with our side. Tristan did not take evasive action, much to my surprise, given he was the Earl's official driver. I screamed and grabbed the wheel as the ute grazed our car's side.

Thanks to my quick thinking, if I do say so myself, we managed to pull out of the ute's way. However, we did end up in a ditch with smoke wafting out of our car. The ute didn't stop.

"Do you know them?" Tristan asked as we both scrambled from the car. "Did you see the driver?"

"No, I didn't see the driver. Whoever it was, was wearing a coat and a huge hat. Plus, it was an old white ute, and ninety percent of the local farmers own an old, white ute. Did you get a good look at the driver?"

Tristan shook his head. "That was a close call. That was definitely on purpose, wasn't it?"

"Definitely," I agreed. "There's no mobile phone service here, so I can't call for help. Let's get out of here before they come back. On second thoughts, let's cut across the paddocks. We'll be safe off the roads if the ute comes back. Watch out for snakes though."

Tristan didn't need me to tell him twice. We both scooped as many tomatoes into our arms as we could and started to walk through a muddy paddock. The tomatoes kept dropping like breadcrumbs in a fairytale, but neither Tristan nor I felt like picking them up.

Cressida was in the front garden, pouring the contents of last night's hot water bottle on a bunch of drooping violets. In a drought, every drop counts. "Do you have my tomatoes?" she said by way of greeting.

"There's a bigger problem," Tristan said. "We had an accident."

Cressida gasped. "Lord Farringdon told me something bad had happened, but I thought he was referring to my tomatoes. What happened?"

Tristan frowned. "I thought Lord Farringdon was your cat?"

I had no idea how to respond, so I addressed Cressida. "Just a stupid driver. We ended up in a ditch," I said. "Are these the tomatoes you wanted?"

"Absolutely," Cressida said. She pointed to the kitchen door as Tristan scooped the tomatoes out of my hand and then vanished.

"I didn't recognise the ute," I said as Cressida patted my shoulder. "It was scary."

"I'll call somebody to tow the car and fix it. Have you called Blake?"

I shook my head. "There was no mobile service out where it happened, and then I didn't have a hand free as I was carrying the tomatoes."

Cressida shook her head. "First the Earl, and now possibly another murder attempt. Are you okay, Tristan?"

Tristan had returned to the front garden. I hadn't noticed before, but his face was bright red. I felt bad for not paying more attention to him earlier. He was, after all, the person who was driving.

"Did you need to sit down?" I asked him.

"I'm fine," he replied, not looking fine at all. "I just need—"

There was a loud noise, and Tristan jumped to the side.

He moved just in time. Something, I assume a gargoyle, fell off the roof and shattered right in front of me—right near where Tristan had been standing seconds before. Tiny shards of plaster rained on us. I screamed and so did Cressida.

We all stood, frozen to the spot.

It took me a moment to come to my senses. "Let's get inside!"

Cressida grabbed Tristan's arm and led him into the sitting room. I followed. "I don't understand. Those gargoyles are firmly attached."

"I'm going up to the roof."

Cressida blocked my way. "It's not safe, Sibyl! This was no accident. The perpetrator might still be up there."

"If I see anybody, I'll run the other way." I should not have gone to the roof, but adrenaline was coursing through me. On the way up the narrow stairs to the roof, I grabbed an antique walking stick that had a sword hidden inside the shaft. It was a novelty item Cressida's ex-husband had given her on their wedding day. He'd regretted that later, although he did live to tell the tale. I took out the sword and tried to breathe deeply as I stepped out onto the roof.

The air here was dusty, the small breeze whipping up minuscule particles of dirt that irritated my throat. I was distracted for a moment by the scenery. The land stretched out, dry and parched, to the hills on the horizon. On one side, the paddocks displayed a slight tinge of green due to the bore water, and there was not a human in sight.

It was easy to walk up here, given the area

directly behind the balustrade was flat. There was nothing for me to slide off, but I kept a tight grip on the walking stick and an eye out in case somebody appeared, intending to throw me over the balustrade.

I moved to the first gargoyle to inspect it. Its base was wide and concrete. How would somebody move a gargoyle? Surely it would take a powerful electric tool and a lot of noise to cut a stone gargoyle loose.

I gingerly moved forward to inspect the gargoyles, but they were all in place. I was perplexed. I had assumed a gargoyle had fallen, but there was nothing else made of stone up here that could fall.

I walked around, checking, but not a single gargoyle was missing. What then, had fallen, narrowly missing Tristan?

Someone had run us off the road, and in hindsight, it was obviously intentional. Then someone had tried to crush Tristan, but with what?

The walk home had taken us a long time. Long enough for the person driving the white ute to arrive here and go up to the roof. I had no idea where the person would have parked the ute.

Maybe they had parked it down one of the side roads, and then hurried here, to the roof.

Somebody wanted Tristan dead.

I took out my phone and called Blake. "I'm all right..." I began, but Blake cut me off.

"I'm coming over now," he replied.

"But I haven't told you what happened yet."

"I figured it wasn't good."

"Someone tried to kill Tristan," I said ten minutes later when Blake stepped into the sitting room.

I had already explained to Cressida and Tristan about the gargoyles, and then I explained to Blake about the fallen object and the white ute. His brow grew more and more furrowed as I went on, and after I finished speaking, he wrapped his arm around my shoulders.

"Did you see anybody?" he asked.

I shook my head. "And we didn't want to leave the sitting room until you got here. We have no idea where the others are."

"Stay here. I'll be right back." With that, Blake disappeared through the door.

A minute or so later, Mr Buttons and Albert burst into the room.

"Are you all right?" Albert asked me in his

Australian accent. His eyes fixed on Tristan, and he gulped. Tristan did not appear to have noticed.

"The target was Tristan," I told him. "We thought one of the gargoyles had fallen, but I went up onto the roof, and all the gargoyles are intact."

"Blake told us to come in here and wait for him," Mr Buttons said. "He will get to the bottom of it."

"Did you see anyone at all?" I asked them.

Mr Buttons and Albert looked at each other. "No, Albert and I were polishing the silverware in the kitchen," Mr Buttons said. "We didn't hear so much as a sound."

I didn't like to ask about the other guests in front of Tristan, but surely it should be obvious to him that one of them was the perpetrator. Even if he didn't trust Mr Buttons, Mr Buttons had been in Albert's sight the whole time.

"Do you know where Jemima, Lavinia, and Tommie are?" I asked Mr Buttons.

"The Englishwomen have been skulking around in the most suspicious manner," Albert said with a wave of his hand.

Mr Buttons gasped and hurried over to Tristan. He pulled a white linen embroidered handkerchief from his pocket and pulled Tristan's hair.

"Ouch!" Tristan said. "What are you doing?

"There were some large particles of an odious substance in your hair," Mr Buttons said. "You can rest easy now. I have retrieved them." He walked over to the fireplace and flicked the particles into the fire.

"So you didn't see Lavinia, Jemima, or Tommie?" I pressed them.

Albert shook his head. "I haven't seen them. Have you, Mr Buttons?"

Mr Buttons had returned to us and was folding his handkerchief carefully into corners. "I haven't seen anybody, not during the entire time it was taking us to polish the silverware. How long has that been, Albert?"

"Too long," Albert muttered darkly.

"What exactly were the Englishwomen doing?" I asked Albert.

"Skulking, lurking."

"Could you be more specific?" Cressida asked, an edge to her tone.

"They seem to appear in odd places at odd times," Albert said with a shrug.

"They wouldn't hurt me," Tristan said.

I sighed. I didn't want to point out the obvious. "Would Jemima, Lavinia, or Tommie want to hurt you?"

Tristan appeared affronted. "Of course not!"

"Then who ran us off the road? And who pushed something over the roof that narrowly missed you? You could have been killed."

Tristan's face flushed red. "I suppose, when you put it like that." He leant forward and put his head in both hands. "I can't believe it! First Peregrine—and now the murderer is coming after me."

Blake stepped inside the sitting room, his expression grim. "I've called the detectives. Tristan, it looks as though a large tile was dropped from the rooftop."

"A tile?" I repeated. "What sort of tile was it?"

Blake shrugged. "I have no idea. It looks like it's a large ceramic tile. Or rather, it *was* a large ceramic tile," he amended. "Cressida, Sibyl, can I speak to you both outside for a moment?"

We slipped out of the room and followed Blake to the end of the corridor. "Cressida, did you have tiles in storage?" He spoke in hushed tones.

"I have some spare bathroom floor tiles in the

tool shed out the back," Cressida said. "I had the main downstairs bathroom remodelled some years ago, and there were leftover tiles. I keep them in the shed."

"How heavy are they?" Blake asked her.

"The tilers left them in the hallway outside the bathroom, and I was able to carry them out to the shed all by myself," Cressida said. "Mr Buttons was somewhere else for the day, and I didn't want to wait for him to help me. I wouldn't have been able to carry two at once, but I was able to carry one at a time. The tiles were quite heavy, but I managed."

I knew where Blake was going with this. He nodded. "Any of those women could have carried one of those tiles up the stairs. Okay, I need to speak with Tristan. Sibyl, Cressida, it's important that you don't mention those spare bathroom floor tiles to any of the guests."

When we were back in the sitting room, Blake came straight to the point. "Tristan, do any of your associates harbour a grudge against you? Jemima, Lavinia, or Tommie would have been able to carry a tile up the stairs."

Tristan leant forward once more. "I can't believe one of those girls wants to kill me."

"Let's not jump to conclusions," Blake said. "The detectives will presently take statements from you all. Leave it to them to do the investigating." He shot me a pointed look.

Tristan took a large gulp of water. "But who could want to hurt me?"

"Why don't you tell us?" Blake said, his voice edgy.

"I don't know. I didn't think I had an enemy in the world."

Blake folded his arms over his chest. "Clearly, somebody doesn't agree with you."

CHAPTER 8

I woke up and yawned. I could see it was a sunny day, given the light peeking around my curtains. To city people, sunny days were wonderful, but in the country, not so much. We certainly needed rain. I allowed myself a small moment of disappointment at the weather and stepped over Sandy's sleeping body. I opened my bedroom door and gasped at the sight in front of me. I stood there in shock.

As I hadn't had my morning caffeine hit, it took me a few moments to process the scene before me. Cressida was asleep on my sofa, and Mr Buttons was asleep on my yoga mat. Of course, he had put a pristine sheet on top of the yoga mat.

I staggered over to the coffee machine, remembering how the two had spoiled my dinner date with Blake the previous night, saying they were too scared to stay at the boarding house with the murderer, so they wanted to stay with me. The fact that Blake *also* wanted to stay with me had entirely escaped their collective notices.

I switched on the machine and leant back against the kitchen sink. The churning sound of the coffee machine must have awoken Mr Buttons, as he sat bolt upright. "Good morning, Sibyl. I trust everything is all right?"

"Yes, everything is fine thanks, Mr Buttons." *Except my love life*, I added silently.

"It was ever so good of you to allow us to stay here last night, Sibyl," he said. "If somebody else is murdered, then Cressida can say I wasn't out of her sight all night, and she could hardly stay in my bedroom at the boarding house. That would be *most* unseemly."

I bit back a smile. "Most unseemly indeed," I said, trying not to chuckle.

Cressida awoke herself with a loud snort. She looked around groggily. "Has anyone else been murdered?"

"Not as far as I know," I said. "I'm making us all some coffee."

Max chose that moment to fly in. "What a &*%& pack of losers," he said before flying out.

I simply shook my head. Sandy walked out of my bedroom and gave me a pointed look. "Okay, I'll give you your breakfast now." Labradors were always hungry, even if they had eaten only moments earlier.

I scooped up a measure of dog food from a container under the kitchen sink and walked to the front door. Sandy ran past me, shaking with excitement. I deposited the food in her dog bowl on my front porch. I wondered why Labradors always ate as though they were starving. While I was I waiting for her to finish her food, I idly looked up at my dog grooming van.

I gasped.

The front door was hanging open. I ran back inside. "I think I've been robbed!" I exclaimed.

Without bothering to explain anything, I grabbed my sneakers and slapped them together hard, before upending them so any spiders or young snakes inside would fall out. This was a necessary Aussie ritual for those living out in the bush.

I slipped on my spider-free, snake-free sneakers and sprinted for the van. I didn't keep any cash in my dog grooming van, so I wondered what somebody could possibly steal. Any expensive equipment was attached to the van and couldn't be stolen.

I breathed a sigh of relief as soon as I ascertained that there were no dead bodies in there and that nothing was damaged. For a horrible moment, I had wondered if someone had broken into my van to deposit a dead body inside.

Mr Buttons and Cressida appeared behind me. "What happened?" Mr Buttons said.

"I saw my door was open, but I can't see anything damaged. I'm perplexed."

Cressida stuck her head inside the van. "Go through all your stock and see if anything's been stolen."

I wondered why anyone would drive out of town to steal my supplies. The first things I checked were my clippers, but they were all there. I checked all my pet shampoos and conditioners on the wall—everything looked fine.

I moved through to the back storage area where I kept the extra stock. "That's so strange," I said, more to myself than to anybody.

"What is?" Mr Buttons prompted me.

"All my coat brightening shampoo is missing. The matching conditioner bottles are missing too. In fact, I recently ordered a large box of them, and they were over there." I pointed to the now empty corner.

"What are they used for?" Cressida asked me.

"They remove stains from white dogs. I mainly use them on white show poodles," I told her. "It gives a silvery effect to a white coat and helps get the stains out. You know all the red dirt we have around here?" They both nodded. "Dogs will always get those red stains on them, and if it's a white dog, then these products remove the stains and make the dog shiny white. You have to be careful though, because if you use too much, it will turn the dog blue."

"Blue?" Mr Buttons said in horror. "That wouldn't do. That wouldn't do at all."

I readily agreed. "I certainly wouldn't want a white show dog to turn blue. Why, the owners would kill me!"

"But why would somebody want to steal that vast amount of product?" Cressida said. "You said a small amount works, but they have taken enough to do probably one hundred dogs."

"The thief took enough to do more than a hundred dogs, that's for sure." I rolled my eyes. "I'll have to call Blake."

It went straight through to voicemail, so I left a message.

"I wonder if this has anything to do with the murder," Cressida said.

"My good woman, how could a theft of coat brightening shampoo and conditioner have anything to do with the murder?" Mr Buttons asked.

Cressida pursed her lips. "I have no idea, but just because I don't have any idea doesn't mean it isn't the case."

I was confused by her words, and apparently so was Mr Buttons, as he scratched his head.

"Let's go up to the boarding house and have breakfast. You too, Sibyl." Cressida indicated her face. "I feel naked without my make-up. Albert can make us a lovely big breakfast, and you can wait for Blake to call you back."

It was early. The guests were due to be served breakfast in another hour and a half. We had plenty of time before the chef had to busy himself with the guests' breakfast. I held my breath as we walked towards the boarding house, hoping we would not be greeted by one of the guests saying somebody else had been murdered. Still, all was quiet.

"How are we all zee morning?" Albert said in his best fake French accent.

I had given up commenting on his accent. The delightful smell of burning wood filled the air. I walked over to stand by the combustion stove. Cressida had an electric oven and electric hotplates in the kitchen, but Albert liked to run the combustion stove. In the old days, it had heated the house's water. These days, the heating too was electric. Still, there was nothing quite like food cooked in a combustion stove.

Mr Buttons at once addressed Albert. "May we assume that nobody else has been murdered, my good man?"

Albert deposited a silver toast rack filled with slices of toast on the table, alongside jars of Vegemite, raspberry jam, and peanut butter. "No, but the tank out by the chook shed has been drained. I noticed it when I let the chooks out this morning."

"Drained?" Cressida repeated in abject horror. "Was it leaking?"

Albert shook his head vigorously. "No, no, no.

It seems as though somebody has used the garden hose. The leak wasn't coming from the tank. The water wasn't around the bottom of the tank but at the end of the hose. Somebody has used the hose in the night, and now the tank is completely drained."

Cressida looked as though she was about to burst into tears. "A dry tank? That is such a disaster!"

Mr Buttons patted her shoulder gently. "No, my dear, it's only the small tank that waters the back garden."

Cressida was practically in tears. "But my plants! My poor plants. They will die without water, and it looks like rain is weeks away. Will it ever rain again?"

"Albert and I will carry buckets from the tank at the front of the house," Mr Buttons said in placating tones.

Cressida at once brightened up. "You will? Does that tank still have enough water for both the front garden and the back garden?"

Mr Buttons hurried to reassure her. "Yes, I'm sure it does, and most of the plants, the azaleas and camellias, are deep rooted. It's only the gardenias that need constant water, and we will pay more attention to those. I wouldn't worry, my dear woman. It was only the small tank that was drained."

Cressida breathed a sigh of relief.

I thought they were missing the point entirely. I spoke up. "Sure, it's bad that the tank's been drained, but why? Why would somebody drain the tank?"

"I supposed the culprit wanted to be nasty," Cressida said. "Why else would somebody do it? Unless they were particularly thirsty." She laughed at her own joke—or rather, what she thought was a joke.

Nobody else laughed. Cressida pushed on. "Somebody was murdered, so there *is* a murderer on the loose. An unhinged, psychotic person who will no doubt commit all manner of crimes!" Her voice rose to a high pitch.

I tried to be the voice of sanity. "But what reason would a murderer have to drain the tank?" I asked. "And you said the culprit drained the smallest tank. It's not as if they drained the front garden tank or the house tank."

Cressida's hand flew to her throat. "Oh my goodness gracious me, you're right, Sibyl. No, this is indeed a mystery. First the murder, then your burglary, and now a tank has been drained."

Albert looked up, shocked. "You were burgled?" he asked, still speaking in his Australian voice.

"Yes, Sibyl has been burgled," Cressida announced theatrically, throwing her hands to the ceiling.

Albert dropped his frying pan with a shock. "Burgled? Streuth! But weren't you staying with her last night, and Mr Buttons too?"

Cressida nodded vigorously. "Yes, but it was her van that was burgled, her dog grooming van, and…"

Albert interrupted her and addressed me. "Was any money stolen?"

I shook my head. "No, I don't keep any cash in the van, and the only movable things were my clippers, but they weren't even stolen. No, it's bizarre—several large bottles of optical whitening shampoo, conditioner, and stain remover were stolen."

"And can such products be used to poison anybody?" Albert asked.

That was a good question, one that hadn't occurred to me. "No, actually, I don't think so," I said. "They are supposed to be perfectly safe if swallowed by pets."

He picked up a fork and turned it over, seemingly studying it. "But what else could it be used for?"

"It's blue in colour. It's used in very small amounts as a stain remover and to give a nice white colour to a dog's coat," I told him.

A look of recognition passed over his face. "Blue, you say?"

"Yes, that's right. Why do you ask?"

He answered my question with a question. "And what happens if too much is used?"

"The dog turns blue."

"Then I know what has happened to your shampoo!" he said dramatically. "There is a blue horse in the back yard."

CHAPTER 9

"My good man, my ears must be deceiving me. What did you say?" Mr Buttons cupped his hand behind his right ear.

"A blue horse. It's a blue horse, I tell you. Large as life and in the paddock behind the house."

Albert hurried out of the back kitchen door, and we all hurried after him. Immediately to our right was Cressida's land, which curved at an angle behind her house. She intended to sell me a parcel of the land, and I was going to build a house on it. Still, we had only broached that subject recently, and the murder had put paid to any further discussion.

Directly behind the house, a little to the left, was another farmer's land. That farmer kept a flock of Merino sheep and a few Hereford cows. We walked to the now-drained tank and stood there in shock.

There indeed was a bright blue horse eating a pile of lucerne hay. Some of the sheep were helping the horse eat, and the Hereford cows were not in sight.

"Did you buy a horse, Cressida?" Albert asked.

"Of course not!" Cressida said. "If I had bought a horse, I would have put the horse on my land."

"More to the point, the horse is blue," Mr Buttons said.

"Yes, that's what I was trying to tell you!" The chef jumped from one foot to the other.

"Then that's what happened to all my products." I pointed to a pool of blue water on the other side of the fence. "The garden hose reaches just through there. Someone has brought that horse to the fence to wash her, and they've obviously not known how to use the product and therefore made the horse blue."

"And there's a blue rug on the horse," Cressida said. "You think they would have purchased a rug in a different colour." She tapped her chin. "Yes, some contrast would be good, something to draw the eye. As it is, there is now an entirely blue horse, and there is nowhere for the eye to rest." Cressida tut-tutted and continued to mutter about art.

Mr Buttons and I exchanged glances.

"Why would somebody steal my products to turn a horse blue?" I asked.

"I haven't seen a horse there before," Albert said. "I would have noticed because I'm the one who always waters the back garden."

"And somebody has fed the horse right on your boundary, Cressida." I nodded to the hay.

Mr Buttons put one finger to the side of his mouth. "Curiouser and curiouser."

"Does anyone know what this could mean?" I asked hopefully but was met with blank faces.

"I have to speak to the people who own that land," Cressida said.

"But they wouldn't come all the way to your house to feed the horse here," I protested.

Cressida waved one hand at me in dismissal. "No, of course not, but if anyone can shed light on the blue horse, it would be them. Maybe it was a prank intended for them."

We all traipsed back inside. Too much had been happening, and none of it made sense. Was the blue horse connected in some way with Peregrine's murder? I had no idea.

What possible motive would someone have to break into my van and steal all those products, simply to turn a horse blue? As hard as I tried, I couldn't come up with a single answer.

"When are we going to visit the farmer who owns that land?" I asked Cressida.

Albert was the one who responded. "I'm not staying alone with these English murderers," he said. "I have to serve them breakfast. Would you please stay and have breakfast with them first and then go talk to the farmer afterwards?"

"I suppose so." Cressida's tone was reticent.

I tried to console her. "We'll be able to think better on a full stomach. No one can ever think when they are hungry. And besides, we might get a clue from the murderers, um, I mean the guests."

"Surely you don't think they were all in it together," Mr Buttons protested.

"No, but something very strange is going on."

Mr Buttons acknowledged my words with a slight incline of his head. After I spoke, I did consider the fact that maybe they were all in it together. It was entirely possible.

Soon, we were sitting in the dining room. The guests had not yet appeared. I was sipping coffee and trying to soothe my nerves. I looked up and noticed the most horrendous painting hanging directly opposite me. Mr Buttons must have noticed it at the same time, because he at once exclaimed, "Cressida! Is that a new painting?"

She beamed from ear to ear. "Yes. I hung it there to cheer up the guests. I took down the other one that was there and put it in my artist studio. This one is more colourful, and bright colours always cheer people up, don't they? Do you like it?"

"It's, um, unusual," I said, narrowing my eyes and focusing them on the frame so that the painting looked blurry, and I couldn't make out the intimate details of people being disembowelled. "What is it, exactly?"

"I call it 'Justice,'" Cressida said. "So many people in the world have suffered injustice, and so vultures have flown down from the mountains to disembowel all the perpetrators of injustice." She beamed widely as she spoke.

I looked at Mr Buttons, hoping he would say something, but his porcelain cup was halfway to his mouth. He sat frozen in horror, as if turned to stone by Medusa herself.

"Well, do you like it, Mr Buttons?" Cressida prompted him. "You haven't said anything."

Mr Buttons took a moment to recover. "It is indeed unique," he said finally.

Cressida clasped her hands with delight. She would have said more, but the door opened, and the suspects filed in—or should I say, Lavinia, Jemima, Tommie, and Tristan all walked in. They took their seats at the table.

Cressida sat, too. "I trust you all had a lovely night's sleep?"

Lavinia burst into tears. She pulled some tissues from her pocket and held them over her eyes.

"Cry baby," Jemima muttered. Even though she had only spoken two words, I was certain they were slurred. I wondered if she had been up all night drinking.

There were already boxes of cereal on the table, and the chef came in and deposited toast.

"Zee cooked breakfast will only be zee minute longer," he said before leaving the room.

Tommie took a piece of toast from the toast rack and offered it to Tristan.

"No, I'm not eating anything that I haven't bought," he said churlishly. "People are trying to kill me, if you hadn't noticed."

He was clutching a large plastic recyclable bag to his chest. He opened it and produced several packets of potato chips, two sports bars, and two triple strength, coffee-flavoured, plastic bottles of milk. He caught my eye and said, "I'm not taking any chances."

I thought he looked pretty good for someone who hadn't had any sleep. "Did you get plenty of sleep?" I asked him.

He looked aghast. "Oh no, of course I didn't! Somebody is trying to kill me! I moved a chest of drawers across my door after I locked it, and I locked the window. I slept on the floor in case somebody climbed up the ladder to the window and tried to shoot me in the bed."

"I see," was all I could manage. For somebody who had spent such a sleepless night, he sure looked quite rested. I wondered if I had dark circles under my eyes and a pinched expression on my face. I supposed I did.

"The police called early this morning. They want to talk to all of us again today," Tommie announced. She appeared to have no worries about being poisoned, because she was slathering margarine over her toast.

Lavinia sobbed even harder, and Jemima produced a hip flask and topped up her coffee with it. She proceeded to slurp her coffee noisily.

"Does anyone know anything about a blue horse?" I asked them.

Lavinia stopped sobbing momentarily. "Did Cressida paint it?" She appeared alarmed.

"No, there's a real live blue horse out the back," I said gesturing with my hand, "and my van was burgled last night. Products were stolen."

"I'm not sure I make the connection," Tristan said.

"Trust me, it's hard to make a connection with any of this," I had to admit. "The products that were stolen would turn a grey horse blue if they were used in sufficient quantities. The horse in the back paddock has recently been washed with these products, and all the water has been drained from a tank."

Mr Buttons leant over to Tristan. "Australians, that is, the ones who live far from town, don't have running water." He wiggled his bushy eyebrows.

Tristan stopped crunching a potato chip. "You don't have water?"

"Not *town* water," I explained. "We have to catch the rainwater in tanks."

Jemima drained her coffee in one gulp and then poured the rest of the contents of the hip flask into the empty cup before draining that too. "So how do you get water for the showers?"

"The rainwater gets caught in tanks," I said patiently. "The water in this boarding house is entirely dependent on the rain. We're very careful with water here, but somebody drained the tank and washed the horse with the products they stole from me, turning the horse blue."

"Do you know why?" Tommie asked.

"I don't have a clue," I said.

Cressida stood up abruptly, spilling her English Breakfast tea.

CHAPTER 10

"We need to solve the mystery of the blue horse at once," Cressida announced. "We will go and speak to the owner of that land and ask if they know anything about the blue horse."

"Why don't you call them instead of driving to see them in person?" I asked. I wondered why that hadn't occurred to me before.

Cressida shook her head. "They don't have mobile service out there."

"Surely they have a landline?"

"Of course!" Cressida hurried to the door. "I'll be right back," she called over her shoulder.

Lavinia was still sobbing softly.

Jemima sighed loudly. "Could you stop that

infernal noise? We're all upset. You're just putting on a big act."

Lavinia turned on her. "What do you mean? Are you trying to imply that I didn't like Peregrine?"

"Oh no, I think you liked him a little *too* in much," Jemima said with a wide smirk.

Lavinia jumped to her feet, her fists curled into balls.

Tommie stepped in between them. "I know you're both upset about Peregrine, but please try to calm down." She patted Lavinia's shoulder. "Jemima, I think we should swap places."

Jemima did not protest, and Tommie took her seat between them. Lavinia kept shooting angry glances at Jemima, but she appeared too interested in eating breakfast.

"What's this black stuff?" Jemima asked. "Oh, it's Vegemite. I've heard a lot about it. Surely, it can't be as bad as they say." She dug a butter knife in the Vegemite jar and spread a piece of toast. Before I could say anything, she stuck a piece in her mouth and then clutched at her throat.

For a moment, I thought she had been poisoned, as she made strangled sounds and dropped her knife. "It is the most foul, disgusting thing I have ever eaten. How can you Australians eat this?"

"You put it on far too thick," I told her. "You're only supposed to spread it thinly on your toast."

She shot me a nasty look. "Whatever."

"Oh Jemima, you're such a b…"

"Lavinia!" Tommie said. "Don't forget you're in company. I wish the two of you would get on." She patted Lavinia's shoulder once more.

"Why do you always take her side?" Jemima snapped. "You two always leave me out of everything. I always feel left out, so is it any wonder I feel upset?"

I thought another fight was about to happen, but thankfully Cressida forestalled it by bursting back through the door. "No, I've lost it!" she announced dramatically, followed by, "Oh no, the fire in the dining room has gone out."

Just then, Albert sailed into the room. "I zee fix eet." He put more logs on the fire and poked them, causing the room to fill with smoke.

"That wood is green!" Cressida said.

I hurried over to the fire, grabbed some firestarter cubes, and threw them on the fire. "This will make the wood burn faster," I said. I flipped the flue to open, and Mr Buttons crossed to the room to open the windows.

"It's too cold to have the windows open," Jemima grumbled.

"I'll shut the windows after the smoke subsides," Mr Buttons told her.

Once the room was free from smoke and the green wood was burning nicely, thanks to half a packet of firestarter cubes and some kindling and newspaper as well, talk turned to the subject at hand.

"I'm afraid I've lost their phone number so we will have to go out and speak to them in person, after all."

"Surely their name is in the book?" Mr Buttons asked.

Cressida shook her head. "No."

"Don't they live next door?" I asked her.

She shook her head again. "No, they have another farm out on the Surrender Road."

My stomach clenched. "Not the Surrender Road? Where all the bogans with rifles live?"

"I know what you're thinking," Cressida said with a dismissive wave of her hand. "They're not like that woman you met out on the Surrender Road. These people are more, um, friendly." She appeared to consider her words for a moment and then added, "And John is a little *too* friendly. Mr Buttons, you will have to come with us."

"Us?" I asked. "Am I coming too?"

"Do you have any dogs booked in for grooming today?" Cressida asked me.

"No." I at once regretted telling her the truth. Maybe I should have said I had five show poodles to clip.

"All right then, let us leave now. Enjoy your breakfast, everyone, won't you?"

I looked at the guests. Jemima and Lavinia were shooting nasty looks at each other, but Tommie seemed to have the matter firmly under control. Tristan was on his fifth bag of potato chips and had downed more than one bottle of coffee-flavoured milk.

I hoped Albert would be able to keep them under control.

I had brought my handbag with me with my house keys in it, given that a murderer was on the loose, so I didn't need to pop back to my cottage to fetch anything.

As we all climbed into Cressida's car, a car sped into the driveway, spraying gravel everywhere. Detective Roberts and Detective

Henderson jumped out. Roberts hurried over to the car and opened the back seat. "Mr Buttons, you are to come with us at once. We need your help with the investigation."

Cressida grabbed my arm, her long bony fingers digging in. The two of us watched in horror as the police led Mr Buttons away.

"We have to find out who did it," she said. "Did Blake tell you anything?"

"Well, he was going to come over last night, but he didn't because you and Mr Buttons stayed over," I said pointedly.

She didn't get my meaning and simply smiled and nodded. "Never mind," she said as we set off to the Surrender Road.

We had to drive into town. We left the dry parched paddocks behind us for the green of Little Tatterford. The residents had town water. They were on water restrictions, but they were allowed to water the garden for two hours every evening. So then, the township of Little Tatterford appeared quite the oasis with green lawns and green trees and shrubs. Of course, native Australian plants didn't need much water, and we passed the resplendent colours of the red bottle brushes, orange bottle brushes, resplendent red and yellow kangaroo paw flowers, and the yellow wattles that were just coming into bloom.

After we drove to the other side of town, we turned off to Surrender Road. That side of town was not as green as the other, and soon we were once more driving through parched paddocks. This was old volcanic country, and huge basalt boulders sat by the side of the road. Some paddocks had barely a blade of grass. "I hope it rains soon," I said to Cressida.

"It will be bushfire season presently," she said, "although there is really nothing to burn, is there?"

I pulled a sad face. We had driven about thirty kilometres, and the scenery was still the same. We were now on a dirt road.

"How far away are they?" I asked Cressida. The dust was finding its way into the car, hurting my sinuses. I hoped I wouldn't get a sinus headache—I could never get those headaches to budge, no matter what I took for them. Putting eucalyptus oil in a diffuser was the best I would be able to do.

"They're down here," she said, gesturing to about twelve old letterboxes all sitting next to each other. She turned left onto a road, which had other roads forking from it. At the end of the long road, she drove up to an imposing blue brick house, one of the typical farmhouses built by the wealthy over a century earlier. The roof was of corrugated iron sheets, and several chimney tops poked up from it.

I figured these people had bore water, not just tank water, because their lawn was particularly green, and the garden was beautiful and lush. I guessed some of the plants mimicked those that would have been originally planted when the house was built: Italian lavender, rosemary, viburnum, grape hyacinth, flag iris, and winter honeysuckle, surrounded by a bed of peonies, bluebells, and jonquils.

I waited for Cressida to get out of the car to see if any dogs would rush up to us, but none did. As I followed Cressida to the back door—it wasn't the done thing to go to the front door on a farm—I could see farm dogs down the back. They all barked at us. Despite the green of our immediate surroundings, the air itself smelt dry, filled with dust as it was.

Cressida knocked on the door, a green-framed flyscreen door opening onto a porch, behind which was a closed, white wooden door. I hadn't noticed there was a dog door in the white wooden door, but it opened and a blue cattle dog ran out. I held my breath. Blue cattle dogs were notoriously territorial and highly protective of their owner's possessions. The dog was not blue like the horse, but a speckled grey colour with black patches.

Thankfully, a man soon appeared behind the dog. "It's all right, Bluey," he said to the dog.

The man opened the flyscreen door and smirked from ear to ear. "Oh, it's my beautiful neighbour, Cressida, and who is this lovely young friend of yours?"

"I'm Sibyl Potts," I said.

He beamed at us. "Come in and have a cup of tea."

"This is John," Cressida said to me.

John laughed and led us into the kitchen. "Judy is just making some morning tea."

Judy frowned at us and then smiled. It appeared to be a forced smile. She was short with a businesslike air about her. Her husband was tall with a bright red face and a bulbous nose. "Hello, Cressida," she said. "I haven't seen you for a while."

Cressida introduced me. "This is my friend, Sibyl. She rents the cottage from me."

"Sit down," Judy said. "How do you have your tea? Or would you like coffee?"

John, who was standing behind her, shook his head at the mention of coffee. "Cressida doesn't like instant coffee," he said. "You had better make her some tea."

"Black with two sugars, please," Cressida said.

"I'll have the same, please," I said.

Within minutes, Judy had laden the table with freshly baked scones, a freshly baked loaf of bread, and chocolate chip cookies. "Would you like an early lunch?" she asked Cressida.

"Thank you, but we had breakfast not long ago," Cressida said.

I knew in the country it was impolite to come straight to the point before eating, and I also knew it was impolite to refuse an offer of a cup of tea and the food that went along with it. After we had eaten, Cressida finally came to the point. "The reason I've come here today is because of the paddock behind me."

John was concerned. "Are the sheep and cattle all right?"

"Oh yes…" Cressida began.

"And the big dam's fine, isn't it? I checked it the other day. There's a bore on that dam and the pump was working when I checked it."

"No, the bore's fine, and the dam's fine, and the sheep and cattle are fine, as far as I know," Cressida said. "No, it's the horse."

John and Judy exchanged glances. "The horse?" they said in unison.

"The blue horse."

"Blue horse?" John said in his booming voice. "Do you mean a grey horse?"

I thought I had better explain. I took a deep breath and launched into it. "I have a dog grooming business. When I woke up this morning, I discovered that my stain removing products had been stolen. Plus somebody had drained the tank at the back of Cressida's boarding house by washing a horse in the stolen products."

John nodded slowly. "Yes, our son had a grey show pony when he was a kid, and we used to use a blue liquid in the final rinse."

I was thankful he understood. "Yes, my products were like that, but whoever did it obviously used too much by mistake, and now the horse is actually blue."

John nodded. "Yes, you've got to be careful with stuff like that, or the animal will go blue."

"But the horse is in your paddock," Cressida said.

Judy did not appear to care about the horse and started clearing the table. I got up to help, but she waved me down.

"We don't have a horse," John said. "I've got my stockhorse stallion and a few mares, but they're all here."

"Do you think one of them escaped?" I asked.

As soon as I said it, I felt foolish. I held up one hand, palm outwards. "Silly me. Your paddocks are miles apart."

"Yes, and I had just come in from feeding them when you arrived," John said. "Besides, I don't have a grey horse. The stallion's bay and the mares are chestnut. One of the neighbour's horses must've fallen through the fence. I had better go and check if a fence is down because I don't want the cattle or sheep getting out. Did you have a thunderstorm out your way last night?"

That puzzled me. "No, why?"

"Sometimes, thunderstorms startle horses and they jump fences, or maybe a tree was struck by lightning and fell across the fence. Did the horse have any cuts and scratches or injuries?"

"No, the horse's legs were perfectly okay—and all blue," I told him.

John moved the butter aside and leant forwards. "What sort of a horse is it?"

"Well, she's a mare about 15 hands," I said. "She was friendly, and she was wearing a blue rug."

"A brand new rug by the looks of it," Cressida added.

John scratched his head. "That *is* very strange. Did it look like a show horse?"

"No, the horse was too thin to be a show horse. Why do you ask?"

"Because I thought some children might have tried to wash the horse, and that's why the horse was accidentally turned blue," John said. "It's beyond me! I could understand the horse getting into the paddock if the fence is down somewhere, but I can't understand why anybody would wash the horse from your tank, Cressida."

Judy came back to the table and sat down. "And wasn't there another murder at your house, Cressida?" There was absolutely no malice in her tone, simply curiosity.

Cressida sighed deeply. "I'm afraid so, Judy. It's a terrible business. The victim was a visiting Englishman."

"Do the police know who did it?" Judy asked.

I was the one who answered. "I'm afraid not."

"Then you two had better be careful," John said. "You don't want to get murdered, especially not by an Englishman. How many Englishmen are still at your house?"

"Only one and there are three English women." Cressida stood up. "Thanks so much for the morning tea, Judy. I'll let you both know if we solve the mystery of the blue horse."

John stood up too. "I'll walk you to your car. That's a nasty business, draining your tank."

"Thankfully, it was only the small tank for the flowers at the back of the garden," Cressida said.

"You have a beautiful garden here," I said.

John pointed to his wife. "That's Judy. She spends all her time baking, knitting, crocheting, and gardening. She's in the Country Women's Association, you see."

We smiled at Judy and then followed John out of the door. As soon as we were outside, he stopped. "It's lovely to see you, Cressida. I'm so happy to see you both. You should drop by anytime." He winked at me. "Do you have a boyfriend?"

I shuddered and opened my mouth, but Cressida answered for me. "Sergeant Blake Wessley is her boyfriend," she said. "Besides, John, don't forget you're married."

"Well, that's never stopped me before," he said in boastful tones. "I've slept with all the women in the local Knitting Association, and the farmer who lives next door has a very attractive thirty-year-old daughter, and she's been making eyes at me."

"Goodbye, John," Cressida said as we hurriedly got into the car. She drove away at speed.

CHAPTER 11

"Motive!" Cressida exclaimed as she swerved to miss a rabbit running across the road.

"Sorry?" I asked when I recovered from being flung forward in my seat.

"We need a motive! The murderer has to be Lavinia, Tommie, Jemima, or Tristan. Jemima is the nastiest one, so she's at the top of my list."

"Jemima was in front of me the whole time." I shut my eyes and tried to recall the events leading up to the murder. "She was the first one who came to look at the painting. I don't think she's the murderer."

"Maybe she had been poisoning the Earl over a period of time," Cressida pointed out.

"Anybody could have placed the bottle of methanol at the scene when we were all in a panic and running around like crazy. Did you see her after we discovered the body?"

I had to admit that I hadn't.

Cressida pushed on. "We need to do two things. Firstly, we need to research methanol—how long it takes to kill, how much is fatal, that sort of thing. And secondly, we need..." She broke off and swung the wheel again, more violently this time.

I flung out my hands to save my head from banging onto the dashboard. "What was it? Another rabbit?"

"No, a kangaroo. A big one, too. They shouldn't be out this late. It's well after dawn."

"Be careful. There will likely be more," I cautioned her. "And roos are hungry due to the drought, so they're moving around more than usual in search of food."

Cressida slowed to a crawl and leant over the steering wheel. "That was a close call."

"What were you about to say?"

She shot me a quick look. "Let me see. Oh yes, I remember. We have to look for a motive."

I readily agreed. "Something occurred to me.

The murderer wants to frame Mr Buttons, so maybe one of the guests has a history with him."

"But he said he didn't know any of them," Cressida protested.

A ute came the other way, travelling at speed. It threw cascades of dust all over us, forcing us now to drive into a thick cloud of red dust. I muttered a few rude words before continuing. "Maybe Mr Buttons had a falling out with one of their parents. It's worth checking into."

"It is indeed," Cressida said, driving even more slowly now. "And we need to uncover any grudges the suspects had against the Earl."

"And I'll ask Blake if anybody reported a stolen horse."

We had now reached the tarred road, so Cressida picked up speed. "Let's drive to the produce store and ask if an English person bought hay."

"And we need to find out where somebody can buy methanol."

Apparently, Cressida knew where the produce store was because she didn't instruct me to look for directions on my phone. It was on the edge of town although down a few side roads twisting this way and that.

Cressida parked the car in a small parking area and then hopped out. I followed her to the front of the brick building where it took the two of us to open a sliding glass door. The woman behind the counter looked up at us. "Are you new in town? I haven't seen either of you before." She narrowed her eyes and tapped her pen on her desk.

"No, no, no," Cressida said. "I'm Cressida Upthorpe, and I own the boarding house out of town."

The woman leant forward. "Oh yes, I know the one. You don't have any horses." It sounded like an accusation.

"No, but there are paddocks behind my house owned by a farmer who lives out on the Surrender Road. This morning, a horse turned up in the paddock right behind my house. The farmer doesn't know who owns her."

The woman gave a little jolt. "I know nothing about a stolen horse," she protested loudly.

I didn't believe her. She was fidgeting and biting her lip, and besides, we had not said the horse was stolen. I wondered why she would lie.

"We have some English boarders staying with us at the moment..."

Cressida would have said more, but the woman cut her off. "Yes!" she exclaimed. "The murder was at your place, wasn't it?" Without waiting for Cressida to confirm, she added, "And all the murders in town have been at your boarding house."

Cressida's face turned a bright shade of red, now matching her heavily applied red blush. "They were all unrelated, I can assure you!"

I interjected before they got into an argument. "The victim was poisoned with methanol."

"Methanol?" the woman repeated. "I wonder why I hadn't heard that yet. The cops must be keeping that pretty close to their chests."

"Do you know who sells methanol in town?" I asked her.

The woman at once looked affronted. "We don't sell it here," she snapped.

I hurried to reassure her. "Oh no, we know you don't, but I figured you'd have a good knowledge of the places people could buy chemicals in town. I mean, I don't even know what it could be used for."

The woman appeared somewhat mollified. "I believe it's used in model aeroplane fuel. Somebody came in here once for some—it was years ago—and I can't remember if it was methanol or ethanol. Actually, I think it was methanol, because at first I thought he wanted to buy metho. We do sell metho here quite cheaply in bulk."

She indicated the five litre bottles of the clear liquid lining the bottom of the shelf to her right. "Maybe you could ask at the local chemist? He might know where you can buy it in town or what it's used for. He might even sell it himself."

Cressida nodded. "Thank you. Anyway, I need to know if an English person came in here and bought hay from you. It was quite good lucerne hay, so I thought it must have been bought from you."

The woman smiled widely. "Yes, we do have very good lucerne hay, top horse quality hay. We also sell cattle quality hay for half the price, but of course, you wouldn't be able to give that to a horse. Lucerne hay is very expensive at the moment," she added defensively, "because they've cut the water allocations to all the lucerne farmers in Tamworth."

Cressida nodded slowly. "A terrible thing," she said. "I heard it on the news. I wonder why they did that?"

The woman stood up. "Why, it's the drought, of course! We desperately need rain. Now, I'm not quite sure what you're asking me. Are you asking whether someone from England, someone with an English accent, came in here to buy lucerne hay from me?"

I nodded. "Yes, that's exactly what she was asking," I said. "It's a mystery how this horse turned up, and nobody seems to know anything about her. However, she was eating some lucerne hay, and since we don't have any, someone had to buy it. We think perhaps one of the English guests put the horse in the paddock."

"Why would you think that?" the woman asked.

It was Cressida who answered. "I have a small tank at the back of the house to water the garden there. It was completely drained, and the horse had clearly been newly washed because she was blue."

I thought I had better explain. "I'm Sibyl Potts. I have the dog grooming business in town, and this morning I found someone had broken into my van and stolen all my stain removing products."

The woman once caught my meaning. "Oh

yes, the blue ones. So somebody washed a grey horse and got carried away with the products, and the mare's now blue."

I was relieved I didn't have to explain further. "Exactly."

"Well, I haven't heard anything about a horse," the woman said.

"Maybe we should tell the police," Cressida said to me.

The woman handed Cressida her business card. "You don't need to get the police involved! I'm sure they have better things to do. Write your phone number on the back of this card, and I'll call you the second I hear of anything. This is the only produce store in town, and people will come here if they have a stolen horse."

"But since you're the only produce store in town, then an English person must have bought the hay from here. You're not the only person who works here, are you?"

Deep furrows formed in the woman's brow. "My husband works here, but he doesn't like being bothered when he's working. He's out the back stacking hay at the moment. I'll ask him about the English people and give you a call if he knows anything." She waved the card at us.

"Anyway, whoever fed the horse might have had a barn full of lucerne hay for all you know. And if they didn't, then they might have bought it from a roadside stall."

"People sell hay at roadside stalls?" I asked her.

She seemed surprised by my question. "Yes, haven't you noticed? There are several, mostly on the roads running out of town. It works on an honesty system. People have an iron box out and you can put money in it. It's mostly the farmers growing their own meadow hay though, as it's too dry here to grow lucerne. Of course, there's no irrigation in Little Tatterford, but I've come across one or two stalls where a farmer has bought more hay than they needed, so they put some out for sale. I'm pretty sure there's a roadside stall out your way," she concluded.

Cressida thanked her. "If you hear anything about a missing horse, could you call me at once?"

The woman said that she would. We were back at the heavy sliding door when Cressida suddenly stopped and turned around. "Oh yes, I forgot to mention that the horse is wearing a rug."

"What sort of a rug?" the woman asked.

"Exactly like that one there." Cressida pointed to an identical rug on a model plastic horse nestled between bags of chicken feed and horse pellets at the back of the shop.

Once more, the woman flushed red. "We're the only place in town that sells horse rugs, and I sell a lot of those. I'd say the horse has escaped from the owners. It's funny they haven't noticed the horse missing, but maybe the owners are from Sydney and only come up every weekend. Never you mind, the second anybody comes in here and mentions a missing grey horse wearing one of those rugs, I will be sure to call you at once."

"That's very good of you, thank you," Cressida said. As we walked to the car, the woman wrestled the heavy door open, stuck her head out and watched as we drove off.

"Did you believe her?" I asked Cressida.

Cressida made a strangled sound in the back of her throat. "Of course not! She was lying through her back teeth, that one. Notice she assumed the horse was stolen rather than simply missing? I mean, who steals horses these days? It's not as though we're back in bushranger times."

I had to agree. "Yes, it *is* strange she didn't

assume the horse was simply missing. I find that suspicious."

"You and me both," Cressida said.

"Are we going to drive around and see if there is, in fact, lucerne hay being sold at a roadside stall?"

Cressida shook her head. "No, because we could be driving around for hours before we find one. They do exist though, because I've seen them before many a time. No, we need to find out where somebody can buy methanol. And then we will look at the English people's car to see if there is any hay around it."

"But we won't be able to look in the car boot surely, because they'll have the keys," I pointed out.

Cressida disagreed with me. "No. Sometimes I've bought some lucerne mulch for my garden, and it gets everywhere. Little bits will have flown out around the car. We simply need to look behind the car and all around it. The wind hasn't been too strong today, so if anybody carried hay in that car, then we should be able to see the evidence."

It was a short drive down the hill on the main street to the only chemist in town. Cressida did a reverse angle park and then shook her fist and said a few rude words at the out-of-town motorist who blasted the horn at her. "How do you think I can reverse park if I don't pull into the middle of the road first?" Cressida yelled, but the car had already gone on its way.

We walked into the chemist and were greeted by a perfectly groomed woman smiling widely. "How can I help you ladies?" she asked.

"Do you sell methanol?" Cressida asked her.

The woman's brow furrowed. "Methanol? What is it used for?"

"Poisoning people," Cressida said.

I elbowed her in the ribs and forced a laugh. "Cressida has such a sense of humour. It's used for model aeroplane fuel, but Cressida's niece is doing a homework assignment on it, and we needed to know some details. We don't want to buy any. We're just gathering information to help her with her homework."

The smile was back on the woman's face. She looked over her shoulder and then back again. "The chemist will be free in a moment. I'll ask him to speak with you. He'll have all the information your niece needs," she said to Cressida.

After she left, Cressida patted me on the back. "That was quick thinking, Sibyl," she said. "I suppose we should have had our stories straight before we came in."

"Oh well, it doesn't matter. She believed us. And look, here he comes now."

The man emerged from behind all the pharmaceutical bottles and skirted around the shelves to stand in front of us. "Your niece is doing an assignment?" he asked. "What's it on? Ethanol?"

"No, methanol," Cressida corrected him. "We need to know what it's used for and where it can be bought."

"Surely your niece can google it." The chemist looked somewhat put out.

"Her parents have grounded her and won't let her use the internet for a week," I said. "Cressida, her aunt here, felt sorry for her and said we would do some footwork for her. We intend to google the uses of it, but we want to know if it's sold in town. She needs that information for her assignment," I ended lamely.

The chemist nodded slowly. "We don't sell it here, but they might sell it at the hardware shop."

"And what's it used for?" Cressida asked him. "We know it's used for model aeroplane fuel."

"And racing car fuel," the chemist said. "And it's used in the manufacture of plastics and paint, and windscreen wash liquid as well as antifreeze. It can also be used in homemade alcoholic drinks, although I certainly wouldn't advise it. Now, if you'll excuse me, I'll have to attend to these people over here." He left after a curt nod to both of us.

"To the hardware store, then," Cressida said. "Who would have thought it was so difficult to discover where methanol is sold!"

When we walked into the hardware store, Nathan, the elderly owner with an outrageous combover, greeted us. "Well, if it isn't dear old Cressida," he said, doing his best to straighten up, and staring at her with rheumy eyes.

"Speak for yourself," Cressida said. "Age is only a number."

The man broke into a hacking cough. "How can I help you lovely ladies today?"

"We don't want to buy any, but we wanted to know if you sell methanol here," she said.

"Oh yes, of course. Come with me." He led us down to the back of the shop past all the cans of paint on the left and pointed to a sole bottle of methanol.

"Is it for somebody else?" he asked Cressida.

"What do you mean?" she said.

"You said you didn't want to buy any, but you asked me if I had any."

Cressida nodded slowly. "Oh yes, I'm terribly sorry. I see what you mean. No, we're doing some investigating. You heard somebody was murdered at the boarding house?"

"Yes, I did. How many people have been murdered there now?"

"Never you mind," Cressida said swiftly. "Anyway, the victim was poisoned with methanol. The police found a small bottle of methanol on the table near him. Sibyl, show him the photo."

I pulled my phone out of my jeans pocket, thumbed through it, and showed Nathan the photo.

"I'd better get my glasses on," Nathan said. He hobbled back to the counter ever so slowly and spent what seemed like an age looking for his glasses. Finally, he popped them on his nose. I had to thumb through the photos again.

"No, we don't sell bottles of methanol like that here," he said. "We hardly ever sell any, and it's only in those big bottles down the back. I've never seen a small bottle of that size before."

"Do you think small bottles like that would be sold in this town?" Cressida asked.

He rubbed his chin. "Maybe the chemist sells it."

"We just asked there," Cressida said.

"Maybe they sell it up at the produce store," he added.

Cressida narrowed her eyes. "No, we've just been there too, and they don't sell it. Would anyone else in town sell it?"

Nathan shook his head. "No, certainly not. I don't think so anyway. I think I'm the only one who sells it, and like I said, I only sell it in those big bottles."

"Thanks for your help. I appreciate it," Cressida said. "Oh, I almost forgot. I need to buy some nails."

"How long do you want them?" Nathan asked.

Cressida's eyebrows shot skyward. "I want them forever, of course! Don't tell me you rent nails here!"

Nathan looked shocked. "I mean, do you want two inch nails or shorter ones?"

Cressida chuckled. "I see. About this long." She held up her hand, her thumb and index finger a little apart. "I only need ten."

After the purchase of nails, we walked out of the door. Cressida paused to admire some of the potted plants for sale. I tapped her arm and nodded to the car.

As soon as we were back in Cressida's car, I said, "It looks as though the murderer bought the methanol somewhere other than this town."

Cressida planted her palm on her forehead. "Of course! Sibyl, the detectives haven't even bothered to check out the bottle!"

"What do you mean?" I wasn't sure where she was going with this.

"The police obviously hadn't asked the lady at the produce store, the chemist, or Nathan at the hardware store. We were clearly the first people who had ever asked them about methanol."

It dawned on me. "Then they're not doing a very good job of investigating. Nathan says that sized bottle isn't sold in town, so it had to be procured somewhere other than Little Tatterford. You would think the detectives should have discovered that by now."

Cressida slapped the steering wheel with her

left hand. "Exactly! And that points the suspicion away from Mr Buttons."

"I'll tell him what we discovered and see if he can mention it to the police." I wiped my hand over my eyes before realising I was wearing mascara. I probably had long streaks down my face. "What do we do now?"

"We look around the English people's car for evidence of hay," Cressida said.

As we drove down the dirt road approaching the boarding house, I caught Cressida's arm. "The grey horse!" I said. I pointed off to the left. "The horse is down there now."

Cressida swung the wheel sharply, causing me to be flung against her. I straightened myself up.

"Sorry about that, Sibyl," she said. "I want to take a closer look."

We drove down the laneway, and I was surprised to see the horse was eating a big pile of lucerne hay. The horse nickered softly when she saw us.

"Someone is now feeding the horse down here," I said. I looked around me. "There are no houses overlooking this area, and we can't see it from the boarding house. What's more, whoever did it would get a good view of the road in both directions."

"That horse obviously isn't simply missing," Cressida said. "Somebody has put the horse in this paddock. I mean, that was obvious by the fact somebody fed the horse in the first place."

Cressida looked around her. "This paddock does have a spring fed dam, and there's underground water here which is why it still has some feed in it, unlike most other paddocks in the entire area." She twirled around and waved her arms expansively.

We drove the short distance to the boarding house, and Cressida parked next to the Earl's car. I looked up at the boarding house to see if anyone could see us, but nobody was looking out the windows, and there was nobody in the front garden.

"Now let's pretend to chat," Cressida said as we walked behind the Earl's car. "You're not saying anything, Sibyl," she complained moments later.

"What do you want me to say?" I asked her.

"Anything you like, but keep your mouth moving so we can pretend we're chatting," she said.

I was still trying to think of something to say when she bent down and then stood up abruptly. "Look at this, Sibyl! Bits of lucerne hay."

I looked at the ground and then looked at the back of the car. I grabbed Cressida's elbow. "Cressida, look! There are little bits of lucerne hay all over the boot and a stalk is stuck in the boot."

"That's it then! One of the English guests has been feeding that horse."

"Cressida! Sibyl!"

We looked up to see Mr Buttons hurrying down the tessellated pathway from the boarding house, followed by Lord Farringdon. Mr Buttons' face was as white as a sheet. "A terrible thing has happened," he said between gasps for breath.

My hand flew to my throat. "Has somebody else been murdered?" I asked breathlessly. "Is it Tristan?"

He shook his head. "No, but the detectives told me I should think about getting a lawyer! Those jolly bad English guests told the detectives that the Earl and I were long-term enemies and had a long-running feud. The detectives are certain I did it."

CHAPTER 12

"Does it have a taste?" Cressida asked.

I tapped away at my laptop and shrugged. Cressida, Mr Buttons, and I were in the kitchen, drinking English Breakfast tea with Albert and researching methanol.

I waved to them to be quiet. Blake had just called me. "I checked for any stolen or missing horse reports, and a local man reported his pale palomino mare missing."

I chewed the end of one fingernail. "This horse is a mare, but she's grey. Are there any other reports?"

"No, but the man who reported the missing horse lives not too far from the boarding house."

"That's strange. Still, the lady from the

produce store hasn't heard anything, and she knows all the horse people. She thinks maybe the grey horse is owned by Sydney weekend farmers who haven't noticed her missing yet."

"That makes sense. Look, Sibyl, I have to go. I'll see you later." With that, he hung up.

"It says here that a large dose will kill somebody quickly," Mr Buttons said.

Cressida jumped up to look over his shoulder. "How fast?" she asked. "The Earl looked perfectly normal, and then before we knew it, he was dead in an instant." She raised her hands and clapped them for emphasis.

Mr Buttons frowned at her. "My dear woman, that is precisely what I'm trying to tell you. It says here that a dose of between twenty and one hundred and fifty grams will be fatal."

"But didn't the liquid look normal and golden?" I asked Mr Buttons.

"It did indeed," he said. "That seems to suggest that the Earl had to drink a quantity of the liquid before somebody added the poison."

"Maybe somebody offered to refill his glass," Albert said.

I thought about it and then disagreed. "No, because methanol is colourless, and the Earl would have noticed if he was suddenly drinking a colourless drink."

Cressida tapped her chin. "You do have a good point, Sibyl. It seems as though somebody poured methanol into his glass after he'd consumed only around half the contents."

"So he wasn't doing shots but simply sipping the tequila," I said.

Albert nodded. "He *is* English." He cast a look at Mr Buttons. "I just meant that Australians are uncouth, as you always say, and the English are far more polite. No offence, Mr Buttons."

"None taken." Mr Buttons looked confused and added, "I'm not sure I understand the insult anyway."

"Okay then, so somebody topped up the Earl's drink with methanol, which we have discovered is odourless and tasteless." I would have said more, but Mr Buttons held up his hand to forestall me.

"On the contrary, this website says methanol tastes bitter. I assume the tequila disguised the taste."

I nodded and pushed on. "This website says it takes anywhere from a few hours to thirty hours to prove fatal."

"Maybe they had been giving him small amounts of methanol over time, and this was the big push that did him in," Albert offered.

Once more, I disagreed. "If the autopsy showed that, it would let Mr Buttons off the hook, and the murderer has gone to great lengths to frame Mr Buttons."

Cressida paced around the dining table. Lord Farringdon followed her. "Maybe they didn't check for that in the autopsy. Mr Buttons, what possible reason would one of the English women have to frame you? A family grudge, maybe?"

Mr Buttons threw up his hands in horror. "Not a possible reason on earth, I can assure you, my good woman. No, this is a crime of opportunity or should I say, a framing of opportunity."

I was perplexed. "Whatever do you mean?"

"Think about it, Sibyl. There are four English guests, and we are certain that one of them murdered the Earl. That is a small number of suspects. Of course, the murderer wanted the police to look outside that little party, namely at me. I'm known to have a long-term grudge against the Earl. Also, the murderer used methanol, something that is commonly found in Australian households."

"Not so commonly!" I interjected. "Cressida and I had terrible trouble finding some in town."

Mr Buttons wagged his finger at me. "But find some you did."

"But not in that exact bottle," I pointed out.

"The police don't seem to care about that," Mr Buttons said, "so that can be of no consequence. Of course, if it comes to trial…" His voice faded away.

Cressida pulled out a chair and sat in it. Lord Farringdon at once jumped into her lap. "It won't go to court Mr Buttons," she said. "We won't let that happen, you'll see."

This was doing my head in. "We need to uncover the motive," I told them. "Mr Buttons, you don't know these English people, but did you know their parents? Have you done anything to annoy anyone over the years? Like foreclosed on a debt, shot someone accidentally in a hunting party, rode in front of the Master's horse while foxhunting..." I tried to think of other things that English people might do that could annoy someone.

Mr Buttons looked at me as though I had taken

leave of my senses. "I have done none of those things you mention, Sibyl. I did spend some time searching their families on the internet, and I'm sure that our families have nothing in common. I highly doubt we have ever crossed paths. Why, we didn't even attend the same schools. No, I don't think the murderer has a grudge against me. As I said, I simply think the murderer is framing me for the sole purpose of drawing attention from themselves."

I tapped my finger on the table. "And speaking of motive, let's consider this. What are the usual motives for murder?" I picked up my tea cup and sipped from it.

"Love, money, and revenge," Albert said. He seized a fire poker and stoked the fire in the combustion stove.

I nodded. "Then let's look at love. Maybe Peregrine was having an affair with one of the women."

"Or maybe with all three of them," Albert said. "I've been a pretend French chef long enough to know the ways of the French. If he was a Frenchman, he might well have been having an affair with all three women."

"But he was an Englishman," I said.

"I'm perfectly certain Englishmen can have affairs with more than one woman. That is not the sole prerogative of the French." Cressida frowned deeply. Cracks formed in her heavily applied powder.

"All right then, it could have been love, but if it was revenge, then it will be harder for us to uncover the motive." Something occurred to me. "Mr Buttons, could you do a search to see if there were any public incidents with Peregrine?"

Mr Buttons looked up from his computer. "Whatever do you mean?"

"I mean, maybe there was a court case or something like that."

Mr Buttons tut-tutted. "I'll search for it just for you, Sibyl, but I can assure you that the landed gentry do not air their dirty laundry in public." He continued to tut-tut as he tapped away at the computer.

I pushed on. "And that leaves money," I said. "We need to look at his heirs."

"The police would have already done that," Cressida said.

"Didn't one of them say the Earl didn't have any children or a wife?"

Cressida nodded. "Yes, I do believe somebody said that. Was it Tristan?"

I shrugged. "It doesn't matter who told us, but if that's the case, then maybe one of the guests stands to inherit everything. If so, that would be even more reason to try to throw suspicion onto Mr Buttons." I thought about it and then added, "Well, on anybody else apart from that party of English guests. And Mr Buttons, having known and disliked the Earl, was the likely suspect."

"And I am afraid the police share your opinion," Mr Buttons said. "I have not turned up anything about Peregrine having a disagreement with anybody, but I shall continue to search."

"It seems to me there are two courses of action open to us," I said. "Firstly, we can ask Tristan if he knows whether any of the women were romantically involved with Peregrine. Secondly, we can find out who inherits."

"How on earth would we do that?" Cressida asked.

Silence fell upon us. We sat there, wordlessly, sipping English Breakfast tea and nibbling on cucumber sandwiches—minus their crusts, of course.

It was Mr Buttons who broke the silence. "I

know."

We all looked at him. He pushed on. "We need to procure the phones of the guests and look through all the contacts to see if anybody has been in touch with a lawyer."

"It's a pity we couldn't get our hands on the Earl's phone," I said.

"I am sure the police have that in their possession," Mr Buttons pointed out.

"I wish I had a cleaning lady," Cressida lamented. "A cleaning lady could go into their rooms and snoop through all their belongings." She looked up at me. "Do you think it's too late to get a cleaning lady? Maybe we could tell the guests she comes once a week."

I thought about it for a moment, but then thought it was a bad idea. "I don't think we should take an outsider into our confidence at this late stage, Cressida. I think we need to do this ourselves. We need to sneak around and find the phone. We could do something to distract the guests."

Mr Buttons clapped his hands. "I know! We will hold a wake. A wake for Peregrine. It would be most unseemly to take one's phone to a wake. That would display a distinct lack of decorum."

"But people do it all the time," I pointed out.

Albert leant over the table. "Not English people."

Cressida jumped to her feet, dislodging Lord Farringdon. He meowed angrily and hurried to the kitchen door. Cressida absently crossed to the door, opened it, looked out, and then shut it, locking it behind her. She hurried back to the table and spoke in hushed tones. "Yes, we will hold a wake for the Earl. When it is in full swing, Sibyl and I will slip out of the door under the pretence of fetching more food. We will run outside and climb up a ladder we have placed nearby in readiness and climb into the guests' rooms to look through their phones."

"Why me?" I said. "What if we're caught? Blake will be furious if he finds out."

"He won't find out," Cressida said dismissively. "And the guests will have no reason to leave the sitting room. Mr Buttons, you can run interference for us. Make sure nobody goes out that door. Do anything to stop them."

"You can count on me," Mr Buttons said.

"And what's more, we will go in disguise on the off chance somebody does happen to catch a glimpse of us."

A bad feeling settled in the pit of my stomach. "Disguise?" I repeated through clenched teeth. "If the guests won't leave the sitting room, then why do we need to wear a disguise?"

"Better safe than sorry, Sibyl," Cressida said smugly. "We'll go in disguise, and if anybody sees us, they will simply think we're native Australian animals."

I couldn't believe my ears. This was going from bad to worse. "Native animals?" I repeated. "Have you completely lost your mind?"

Cressida continued to smile. "It will be a good disguise. The English guests are already afraid of Australian native animals, and if they see us, they won't approach us. They will run in the other direction." Her voice rose to a high pitch.

"Australian spiders can be deadly, but they only grow this big," I said, holding up my thumb and index finger a little apart. "And there's no way we can disguise ourselves as snakes. Sharks only live in the water, and crocodiles don't come indoors. What possible scary Australian animal could we disguise ourselves as?" I rolled my eyes.

Cressida continued to smile. "Drop bears!" she said.

CHAPTER 13

I rubbed my eyes with both hands. "This is a joke, right?" I asked hopefully. "There's no such thing as drop bears!"

"You know it; I know it, but the English guests don't know it," Cressida said smugly. "All foreigners are scared of drop bears. We will dress as koalas and break in…"

I interrupted her. "But koalas aren't even bears!"

Cressida shrugged. "No matter. The truth is inconsequential—what matters is that foreigners are terribly afraid of drop bears."

I shook my head. Australians like to scare foreigners with the mention of mythical creatures known as drop bears. They are said to be giant koalas with long pointed teeth. Drop bears are said to drop from trees onto foreigners to kill and eat them. Of course, drop bears aren't real. They are not like bunyips and yowies, actual mythical Australian creatures—drop bears were simply invented in recent times as a joke, purely to scare people who came to this country.

I looked at Mr Buttons for help. "Mr Buttons, what do you think of this idea?"

"I'll leave you two ladies to sort it out between yourselves," Mr Buttons said. He didn't even look up but continued to tap away at the keys.

"But you wouldn't happen to have drop bear costumes, would you?" I asked, fervently hoping that she didn't.

It seemed it wasn't my day. "Yes, I bought two costumes when I was looking for some flameless candles online. I think flameless candles are awfully useful because they give that lovely glow, but if you forget about them, they can't burn your house down." She stopped speaking to grin widely. I wondered when—or if—she would come to the point. "And so I was looking online for some silver flameless candles and some lovely ivory flameless candles. Did you know some even come with remote controls? Anyway, I was looking for some pretty ones, and the candle website took me to a Halloween website. They had lots of costumes, and I was completely taken by two drop bear costumes. I thought I would buy them."

Mr Buttons did speak now. "Good grief! Whatever possessed you, Cressida?"

"Where were you going to wear them?" I asked.

"Nowhere," she announced brightly, "but I thought they would come in handy one day. And I was right, wasn't I!"

Mr Buttons and I exchanged glances. Lord Farringdon scratched on the door, and Albert let him in.

Cressida was still talking. "We'll have a wake for the Earl, ply everyone with alcohol, and Mr Buttons can guard the door. If anybody does see us, we can make scary growling sounds and wave our claws at them."

"But Cressida, they will know at once that we're wearing costumes," I said.

"Sibyl, I don't know why you're complaining. It's not like you to complain so much. No, it's a good plan, and you're to do as I say. Now, let's organise the wake. When should we do it?"

"As soon as possible," Mr Buttons said. "The police could arrest me at any time, so there are time constraints. Albert, is it possible to have a wake this afternoon?"

Albert looked stricken but soon recovered. "We do have plenty of wine. I could easily rustle up some finger food, I suppose. I have plenty of supplies in the freezer." He narrowed his eyes. "Since I've been working here, I've learnt to be prepared for every eventuality."

And so, that afternoon, we found ourselves at the Earl's wake. The wine was flowing freely. I fervently hoped the English guests would soon be too inebriated to get up the stairs. Of course, Jemima was already halfway to inebriation.

"Good, Jemima is blotto," Mr Buttons said.

I agreed. "Yes, she's smashed off her face."

Jemima was sitting on one of the Chesterfields, turning her glass this way and that and giggling to herself. Lavinia was sobbing into a tissue. The one problem with our plan was that Tommie was in bed with a migraine. She would be too sick to emerge from her room and catch us snooping through her friends' rooms, but that meant we would be unable to look at her phone. Still, we could look through Lavinia's, Jemima's and Tristan's phones. I was secretly pleased because it cut my work down by a quarter.

After half an hour or so, Cressida nodded to Albert. He nodded back and slipped out of the door. I knew it was his cue to put the ladder in place. I moved around the room, refilling the guests' glasses with wine. Tristan, of course, had brought his own wine. He was drinking from a plastic wine glass he must have purchased at the local supermarket. I could see he wasn't taking any chances with further poisonings.

Albert stuck his head around the door and nodded to Cressida.

"Come on, Sibyl, help me see to the meal," Cressida said in loud tones. She fixed Mr Buttons with a look. He went to take his place in the doorway.

Once through the sitting room door, Cressida and I ran to the kitchen. The French chef was waiting outside. He held the door open and then shut it behind us. Cressida locked the door, and we changed into the dreadful drop bear costumes as fast as we could.

"It's hard work to move in this," I said to Cressida.

"You're right," came the muffled reply.

"Maybe we should have practised a lot first. Well, never mind Sibyl, no time like the present. Come on, make like a koala. We have a ladder to climb."

"Maybe we should leave the koala slippers in the house," I said. "They're too big, and they'll hinder us when we climb the ladder. Besides, the claws could make a sound on the floorboards in the guest bedrooms."

"You're right," Cressida said. "I'll shove them in the fridge."

"The fridge?" I parroted. *Oh whatever, let Cressida do whatever she wants*, I thought. I just wanted this whole ordeal to be over with.

We slipped out the back door and waddled over to the ladder.

Cressida shimmied up the bottom part of the ladder like a rat up a drainpipe but got stuck half way. I was not so lucky, as her big koala bottom hit my face as I tried to climb the ladder. I tried not to look down, but I was unable to look anywhere at all with Cressida's furry koala behind directly above me.

I have no idea how I made it up the ladder. It was only when we reached the top that I wondered what would happen if the window was shut. To my surprise and enormous relief, it was open. Cressida reached in and pulled me through to the floor. I fell heavily, but the koala costume saved me from bumps and scratches.

"This is Tristan's room," Cressida said. "I'm surprised he left the window open. You'd think someone so scared of being murdered would have left it shut."

I shrugged. "He might have wanted some fresh air," I said, "and he did say he keeps it locked at night."

"There's no time to chat, Sibyl. Let's search the room for any evidence of criminal activities."

"What evidence could there possibly be?" I asked her. "The police already have the bottle of methanol in their possession. If Tristan *is* the murderer, then what else would he have lying around? And besides, somebody's already tried to murder him."

Cressida paused. "Yes, you're right. Then let's simply look for his phone."

I found his phone easily. It was on the chest of drawers next to the window. "Mr Buttons was right. His English friends, or his enemies, whatever they are, really don't take their phones to wakes," I said. I picked up the phone and thumbed through it.

Cressida looked over my shoulder. "Sibyl, do you have your phone on you? Take photos of anything suspicious."

"I certainly do have my phone," I said, "but I can't see anything suspicious here."

"Look at recent calls," Cressida insisted.

I slapped myself on the side of the head with my large paw. "Silly me! Cressida, there are recent calls between Tristan and an English person. Does this sound like a lawyer to you? Travers Markinswell-Weston. No, that's a personal name." I flipped through to the Contacts folder. "There's a business name under it, Wells, Winchester & Weston."

"That could be his stockbroker or anybody," Cressida said. "We'll have to do an internet search for it later, but we can't do it now. Quick, Sibyl, take a photo of it. We have to move on. Mr Buttons won't be able to keep the English guests in that room forever."

I didn't need telling twice. I took my phone out and took photographs of Tristan's recent calls.

Cressida padded closer to me. "Let's slip out of his room and try Lavinia and Jemima's rooms," she said. "One of those women is the murderer, you mark my words."

She produced a master key from her pocket and unlocked Tristan's door. We let ourselves out into the corridor. As Cressida busied herself locking the door, I was left wondering why we hadn't come up the stairs in the first place.

A noise startled me. We both swung around. To my horror, Tommie was sneaking along the corridor. We all saw each other and froze.

"What are you doing coming out of Tristan's room?" Tommie said. "And why are you dressed like those scary monsters?"

"Scary monsters?" I repeated.

"Yes, drop bears," she said.

"I told you the English guests would think we were drop bears," Cressida hissed.

I decided I might as well tell her the truth. "Tommie, whoever murdered the Earl is trying to frame Mr Buttons, and the police are closing in on him. Cressida and I know it wasn't Mr Buttons, so we searched Tristan's room and looked through his phone contacts."

Tommie appeared genuinely puzzled. "But somebody has tried to kill Tristan twice," she said.

"We looked through his phone to see if we could find out who inherits the Earl's fortune, or rather, what's left of it," I said.

A blank look passed over her face.

"Do you have any idea of the identity of the Earl's heir?" I asked her.

"No, I don't," she said. "I only know it wasn't me, but I've never heard anybody discuss it."

Cressida took a step forwards. "And I thought you were in bed with a migraine." Her tone was accusatory.

Tommie appeared to be flustered. "Um well, I didn't really want to go to the wake."

"Then where have you been?" Cressida demanded. "You weren't in your room. You've been outside, haven't you?"

Tommie bit her lip. It took her a few moments to answer. "Yes, I didn't want to go to the wake, but I didn't want to be cooped up in my room either. I wanted some fresh air."

"Would you mind not telling Tristan that you saw us?" I said. "We don't think he did it, but we thought he might know who inherited."

"Why didn't you just ask him?" she said.

"I *have* asked him," I told her. "He said he didn't know, but I think he was lying. If we're to save Mr Buttons from being arrested, then we need to know who inherits the Earl's fortune."

Tommie appeared to be considering the

matter. "All right, I'll keep your secret on the condition you don't tell the others that I didn't have a migraine."

Cressida and I both nodded. "Deal," we said in unison.

CHAPTER 14

Cressida hurried in the direction of the stairs. I followed her, wondering what would happen if the other guests left the sitting room, but I was certain Mr Buttons would do his job well. When we reached the safety of the kitchen door, Albert opened it and looked at us in shock. "How did it go?" he asked us.

I was busy pulling the drop bear costume over my head and didn't hear Cressida's reply. When I finally got it off me, I asked her, "Cressida, why didn't we search Lavinia's or Jemima's room?"

"Didn't you see Tommie? She was standing there, her hands on her hips. She was blocking the corridor, and I'm sure she wouldn't have allowed us to search the other rooms. I think we were lucky as it was."

Albert gasped. "You were caught?"

Cressida scratched her head. "Didn't I just tell you that? Yes, she caught us coming out of Tristan's room. She promised not to tell if we promised not to tell she didn't really have a migraine."

"She didn't have a migraine?" Albert asked.

"No, she was pretending, and I find it highly suspicious." I put my hands on my hips and watched Cressida as she struggled to get out of the drop bear costume. She bundled the costumes into a large striped bag and zipped it up.

"Should we get back and help Mr Buttons?" I asked her.

"No, first of all, we have to call that number."

Albert looked up from his blowtorch. He was setting aflame the delightful sugary top of several crème brûlées. "What number is that?"

Cressida sighed deeply. "Albert, didn't you listen to a thing I said? We found a phone number in Tristan's phone contacts, and we think the name could be a lawyer. I'm going to call England."

I had my reservations. "What excuse are we going to give them?"

"I'll pretend I'm a lawyer acting for Mr Buttons. Besides, if they answer the phone and say they are some other sort of business, I'll simply hang up."

"Set your phone to blocked caller first," I said to Cressida. "You don't want them calling you back."

Cressida nodded vigorously. "Good idea." She turned to her cat, happily asleep in front of the combustion stove. "Lord Farringdon, do you think I should call that number or ask Mr Buttons to do it?" She stared at the cat for a few moments and then said, "Oh, my goodness me, Lord Farringdon! I can't believe you said that. You've spent too much time in the company of Sibyl's cockatoo."

"What did he say?" I asked automatically, before realising he was a cat and wasn't saying anything at all.

"He told me he didn't care what I did," Cressida said. "Lord Farringdon has never been so rude. Anyway, I had better make the call now, because I think we've left Mr Buttons alone for too long."

Cressida turned to Albert. "Are you about to carry those into the dining room?"

"Yes, they're ready now."

"Can they wait a few minutes?"

Albert looked quite put out. "No," was all he said.

"All right, Albert, you take them in, and I'll call the number. Be very quiet when you come back."

Cressida held the door open for Albert as he walked out, carrying a large tray of crème brûlées.

She picked up the phone and trembled a little. "I'm quite nervous, to be honest, Sibyl."

I hurried to reassure her. "Don't worry, Cressida. Just make sure it shows up as a blocked caller and they'll never know who you are."

Cressida nodded and then asked, "And who am I again?"

"Say you're a lawyer acting for Mr Buttons. If they ask for your number, don't say anything and then pretend it's a bad phone line."

Cressida looked at the ceiling. "I'll have to call myself something. What's a good fake name for an Australian lawyer?"

I rubbed my forehead. Try as I might, I couldn't think of a single thing.

"Never mind. I'll make it up as I go along," Cressida said. "What time is it in England?"

I took my phone back from her and looked at the world clocks. "It's just past nine in the morning in London," I told her.

I flipped my phone back to the photo of Tristan's contacts and handed it to Cressida. She set her phone to loud so I could overhear the conversation.

It took a while before somebody answered, and then a female voice said, "Good morning, Wells, Winchester & Weston Lawyers Chambers. How may I help you?"

Cressida and I nodded to each other. It was a law firm, after all!

"Good morning. I am an Australian lawyer by the name of Sheila Dundee," Cressida said. I did my best not to giggle. She pushed on. "I represent a gentleman by the name of Mr Buttons otherwise known as Lord Nithwell, the Fifteenth Earl of Nithwell." She hesitated and took a deep breath before continuing. "Lord Nithwell had a long association with Peregrine Winthrop-Montgomery-Rose-Bucklefort, the Fifth Earl of

Mockingbird, who died recently. Mr Buttons, um, Lord Nithwell, has asked me to contact you to see if he's an heir. The two earls knew each other for years."

"The Earl of Mockingbird, you say?" the woman's voice asked.

Cressida nodded and then caught herself. "That is correct."

"May I put you on hold?"

Cressida gave me the thumbs up. "Certainly."

It was moments before a male voice spoke. "Good morning. This is Travers Markinswell-Weston."

"Good morning, Mr Markinswell-Weston. I am an Australian lawyer by the name of Sheila Dundee. I represent the Earl of Nithwell. My client has informed me that the Earl of Mockingbird died quite recently, and given the two of them had been friends for many years, my client requested I contact you to ask if he was an heir."

"I'm sorry. I'm not at liberty to divulge that."

"But, but, Mr Buttons, um, I mean, I'm the Earl of Nithwell's lawyer! Cressida said, her tone indignant.

"I'm afraid I can only give that information to the Earl or his legal representation."

"But I *am* his legal representation," Cressida said.

"Certainly. If you would fax me the details…"

The man was still speaking when Cressida hung up.

"Mr Buttons himself will have to call them," Cressida said. "Let's mingle with the guests for a short time and then we'll make Mr Buttons call them himself."

Albert came through the door. "Everything seems fine in there, but Jemima is plastered."

Cressida snorted. "What else is new? Albert, are those crème brûlées for us?"

"Yes, those two are, and this one is for me."

"Sibyl, we had better take them out and eat them with the guests."

I agreed with Cressida. We walked to the sitting room, followed by Lord Farringdon who appeared to have forgiven Cressida. "I'll fill in Mr Buttons, and you keep an eye on the guests," Cressida said. "And remember, Sibyl, don't put your food down or leave it unattended. There's a murderer on the loose."

When we reached the dining room, Tommie

and Lavinia were sitting on the Chesterfield, chatting away. When Lavinia saw us, she pulled a tissue from her pocket and dabbed at her eyes. I was beginning to think it was all an act.

Jemima was lying on a loveseat, draped over it at a bizarre angle and was giggling to herself. She was clutching a bottle of wine. Mr Buttons was standing just inside the door eating a crème brûlée. Cressida nodded to him and took him aside over by the chaise. She pushed some of the Japanese Peace Lilies away from the front of it and gestured he should sit there. The two of them put their heads together and spoke in hushed tones.

"Are you enjoying the wake?" I asked Tristan and Lavinia. There was simply no point speaking to Jemima.

Tristan smiled at me. "Yes, it's lovely. Peregrine would have liked it."

"But he's dead!" Lavinia covered her face with a tissue. I ignored her and addressed Tristan. "Are you sure you don't want to try some crème brûlée?"

Tristan gasped. "And risk dying? Absolutely not. It's clear I'm the only other target."

I was puzzled and said so. "Why do you say that?"

"It's obvious, isn't it? Nobody else is dead."

"You do have a point." I noticed he was eating a sandwich. When he saw me looking, he added, "I bought these from a local shop in Little Tatterford. I bought several, and I keep them with me at all times. I can't take any chances. It's obvious the murderer is going to strike again."

"Hopefully, the police will come up with some evidence first," I said. "If you two are happy to chat, Cressida and I will help the chef in the kitchen."

Tristan didn't seem to think my words were suspicious and turned back to Lavinia. I walked over to Cressida. "I've explained everything to Mr Buttons," she said.

I nodded. "I told Tristan and Lavinia we were going to help Albert in the kitchen."

I walked to the door, followed by Mr Buttons and Cressida. As soon as we were out of earshot, I said to them, "Tristan made a good point. He said he must be the only other target, given that none of the women are dead."

"Maybe the murderer is simply biding her time," Mr Buttons said.

Albert unlocked the door to the kitchen and locked it behind us. Cressida handed her phone to Mr Buttons. "You can call from my phone. It's still set to blocked caller."

Mr Buttons wasted no time. "Hello, this is the Earl of Nithwell," he said. "I would like to speak with Travers Markinswell-Weston, if I may."

The woman put him through at once. Mr Buttons introduced himself and then said, "I am here with my counsel, Sheila Dundee. She is having trouble with her phone line, so I hope you can hear me." The lawyer assured him that he could. Mr Buttons pushed on. "Peregrine Winthrop-Montgomery-Rose-Bucklefort, the Fifth Earl of Mockingbird, and I were friends for many years. I would simply like to know if I am one of his heirs."

The lawyer cleared his throat. "No, you are not an heir."

"Good grief man, are you certain? That comes as a surprise. Can you tell me who does inherit?"

"I'm sorry, but I cannot divulge that information," said the disembodied voice. "I can simply tell you that the heirs have been informed."

"All the heirs?" Mr Buttons asked. "Are you certain?"

"Yes, I'm absolutely certain."

"I see. Oh well, good day, old chap." Mr Buttons hung up. To us, he said sadly, "I'm afraid I wasn't any help at all."

I tried to cheer him up. "Never mind, Mr Buttons. I think you did well. The lawyer wasn't going to tell you, no matter what."

Mr Buttons frowned and then said, "But the lawyer would tell the police."

"Yes, surely the police have called them by now," I said. "And notice he said heirs, plural?"

Mr Buttons shrugged. "He would simply say that to obfuscate the matter. One cannot know whether there is one heir or more than one heir. I know, I shall call him back and pretend I'm one of the detectives. That will give me the opportunity to him ask further questions."

Cressida caught his arm. "Mr Buttons, you can't do that. They'll know you're an Englishman, not an Australian."

"Poppycock, my good woman. I've been in Australia for many years, and now I have not the slightest trace of an English accent remaining."

Cressida and I looked at each other. "I'm

afraid to tell you that you sound extremely English, Mr Buttons," I said. "And Cressida and I can't call, because the Little Tatterford cops are all men."

We all looked at Albert. He put up both hands in front of him and backed away. "No way, no way. I'm not calling them."

Cressida pulled some money from her handbag and slapped it on the table. "There's twenty bucks in it for you."

"All right, all right. What do you want me to say?"

"Just tell them you're a detective from the Australian police working with Detective Roberts and Detective Henderson," I said. "They won't be suspicious."

Albert rolled his eyes. "This is ridiculous! What name will I give them?"

"It has to be an Australian name," I said.

"What's a typical Australian bloke's name?" Albert tapped his chin.

"Paul, Bill, Tom, Lachie, John," I said, trying to think of others.

"And what about a surname?"

"I'm sure it doesn't matter," Mr Buttons said.

"You sound Australian, and that's all that matters."

"Matters!" Albert said. "I'll be Matt Matters. Give me the phone before I change my mind." He all but grabbed the phone from Cressida's hand and pressed redial. "Hello, I'm Detective Matters from the Little Tatterford police in Australia," he said. "I'd like to speak with Travers Markinswell-Weston."

"I'm afraid you've just missed him, Detective Matters."

"I see. When will he be back?"

"I'm not sure. Is there something I could help you with?"

We all nodded our encouragement. Albert rolled his eyes and said, "Yes. Mr Travers Markinswell-Weston has spoken with my colleagues, Detective Roberts and Detective Henderson, concerning the case of the murder of the Earl of Mockingbird. I have a question about his heirs."

"His heirs?" she repeated.

"Yes, um, it's all on record, but I'm afraid Detective Roberts who's a bit of a drongo has lost the file. You see, we're quite incompetent out here in Australia at the Little Tatterford police station, not like you Brits."

I put my hand over my eyes. This wasn't going as well as I'd hoped.

"Here is Mr Markinswell-Weston now. I'll see if I can put you through. Please hold."

Classical music blared through the phone for some time before a man's voice spoke. "Good morning, Travers Markinswell-Weston speaking."

"Hello, this is Detective Matters from the Little Tatterford police, um, homicide squad in Australia," Albert said. "I am assisting my colleagues, Detective Roberts and Detective Henderson, in the murder case of Lord Mockingbird. We need to know who inherits Lord Mockingbird's estate."

"I have already spoken to Detective Roberts about that," the lawyer said.

"I'm afraid he's lost the file," Albert said. "And we didn't have it online because we live in a small country town, and so we don't have the internet here. We're backward Down Under, you see, and Roberts doesn't know where he put the file. He would forget his head if it wasn't stuck on."

The line went dead.

"Should I call back?" Albert asked.

Mr Buttons shook his head. "No, I'm afraid not. The game is up, my dear boy. That lawyer knows you were not a detective."

"I wonder how he possibly figured that out?" Albert scratched his head.

"No idea," I said, to make him feel better. "Is there any possible way we could discover who inherits?"

Cressida shook her head. "No, it wouldn't be recorded anywhere."

It was my turn to shake my head. "I didn't mean that. I meant, is there anybody else who knew the Earl well? Mr Buttons, you knew him for years. What about his other friends? Could you call somebody who knew him and ask?"

"I thought of that myself, Sibyl," Mr Buttons said. "I've been out of touch with Peregrine for years, and I'm sure we don't have any mutual friends."

"But you're both Earls," Cressida protested. "Surely you must know someone who knew Peregrine."

"I'm sure I know several people who knew Peregrine," Mr Buttons said, "but that doesn't mean they'll know the identity of his heirs."

Cressida shrugged. "It's worth a shot."

Mr Buttons nodded slowly. "All right. I'll make some calls. But there's something you have all overlooked."

We looked at him expectantly.

"Tristan has been speaking with the lawyer. Surely then, Tristan is one of the heirs."

Albert dropped a cast-iron frying pan. "Mon Dieu!"

CHAPTER 15

The following morning, I was busy playing catch up with my dog grooming clients. Luckily, I didn't have to shampoo any white dogs. I had ordered new products, but they wouldn't come for another week or so. Mail to small country towns in Australia always took ages.

Cressida had hatched a plan to take the English women one by one to a local café in order to question them. I had not wanted to be party to any more of her wild schemes, especially after the whole drop bear debacle of the previous day, not to mention the whole calling the English lawyers debacle.

I'd had enough of Cressida's schemes to last

me for a very long time. I had told her she had to deal with it by herself. I only changed my mind when she called to say Mr Buttons had been taken in for further questioning, and the detectives suggested to him he would need a lawyer.

That meant the stakes were high, and we were under time pressure. I reluctantly agreed to accompany Cressida. Cressida's plan involved telling each Englishwoman we wanted to have coffee with them in turn, ostensibly so we could give each one our undivided attention. Cressida told the women she did that with all her guests.

That part of her plan, at least, I thought was sound. That way we could have the women coming in and out of the café, and they wouldn't be surprised if they ran into each other.

Instead of a coffee shop, Cressida had asked to meet them at the Top Pub. In Australia, the size of country towns was generally measured by the number of pubs. For example, somebody would say, "It's a three pub town." Little Tatterford was a two pub town with a top pub, the north pub, and a bottom pub, the south pub. The Top Pub had a lovely coffee shop, quite private and with a roaring fire. It was there Cressida said we would meet the women.

Cressida picked me up in her car and we arrived at the Top Pub a good ten minutes early. "What are we going to say?" I asked Cressida.

"We will make conversation and play it by ear," she said.

Something occurred to me. "Did you ask them to the Top Pub so you could ply them with alcohol and get more information out of them?"

Cressida smiled. "No, but that's a good idea. It hadn't occurred to me."

Instead of sitting in front of the roaring fire, we had chosen to sit at a corner table overlooking the street. Cressida had said that would be a good vantage point to see who was coming and going.

The fragrance of the lilies in a vase on our table was pungent. I took the vase off our table and placed it on a nearby table. Sometimes, overly sweet floral scents gave me a sinus headache.

I looked out the window to see Tommie drop off Lavinia and Jemima on the footpath. "Oh no, they're together," I said but soon added, "No, it's okay. Jemima is walking away."

Lavinia looked around the room. We were the only ones there, so she spotted us at once.

"Thank you for inviting me," she said. She pulled out a tissue and dabbed it under her eyes. I saw she was wearing a considerable amount of mascara and hoped she didn't forget herself and wipe her eyelashes. I also wondered if her tears were crocodile tears or whether she had genuinely liked Peregrine. Or maybe she was crying because she was the murderer and was overcome with guilt.

A waitress approached. "What can I get you?" she asked.

"I don't think we have decided yet," Cressida said. "Could you give us a few more minutes?"

The waitress nodded and left. I was fairly certain she was one of the owners. I figured the Top Pub didn't get many customers so early in the day, given that their main business was the bar and the restaurant at night.

Cressida turned to Lavinia. "There's the cake stand over there. Go and choose one."

Lavinia wasn't gone long. "They have some lovely cakes," she said.

The waitress must have seen her return to our table because she presently reappeared. We all ordered coffee. Lavinia ordered a lumberjack cake with ice cream and cream, and Cressida and I settled for a slice of lemon meringue pie each.

Cressida leant forward and patted Lavinia's

hand. "You poor dear. It must have been a horrible shock to you, having your boss murdered like that."

Lavinia pulled a bunch of fresh tissues from her handbag.

"Were the two of you close?" I asked.

She shot me a look and then said, "Yes, we were friends."

I wondered if we would be able to get any useful information out of her. It wasn't looking good.

Cressida pressed on. "How long have you known the Earl?"

Lavinia rearranged the cutlery on the table ever so slightly. "A long time," she said.

This was going nowhere. I thought I might as well come to the point. Cressida must have realised what I was thinking because she shot me a warning look. Nevertheless, I asked, "Who do you think did it?"

Lavinia looked up, startled. "Did what?"

"Murdered the Earl," I supplied.

She twisted the bunch of tissues in her hands. "Don't the police think it was Mr Buttons?"

"Of course it wasn't Mr Buttons," Cressida snapped. "I've known Mr Buttons for many years, and he couldn't possibly murder anybody. No, I'm afraid it was one of your party."

Lavinia's face turned a pasty shade of white, and for a moment, I was afraid she would faint. "You're not serious?"

I thought she might run out of the door, so I spoke in soothing tones. "We're just worried about your safety. We know you didn't do it because you're been so upset, but the others haven't seemed quite so upset."

She nodded slowly. The waitress appeared and set our coffees in front of us. Cressida's spilt, so the waitress apologised profusely and made a big show of mopping it up. "We need rain, don't we!" she announced to nobody in particular.

"Oh, it's terribly dry," Cressida lamented. "It's forecast for the end of next week, though."

"It's always forecast for the next week," the waitress said with a sigh before leaving.

I was wondering how to get the conversation back to the subject of suspects, but Lavinia spoke up. "It couldn't have been Tristan. He narrowly escaped being murdered."

I agreed. "So that only leaves Jemima and Tommie."

Lavinia took a sip of her coffee before setting

down her cup and taking a long, deep breath. "I can't sleep at night," she said. "That's what I've been thinking. It must be Jemima or Tommie."

"Do you suspect one over the other?" I asked her.

She looked over her shoulder and then back at us. "Is this completely confidential?"

Cressida hurried to reassure her. "Of course. Do go on."

"Jemima is mean, and she drinks too much."

"I thought the two of you were friends?" I said.

She shook her head. "No, not at all. I mean, I've known Jemima and Tristan for ages. Tristan seems nice enough, but I don't trust him. Jemima was all right at first, but she's been drinking heavily lately."

"And what about Tommie?" I asked her. "When did she start working for the Earl?"

"She only started working for him recently," Lavinia said. "I think she was throwing herself at him."

I was surprised. "Do you mean in a romantic way?"

Lavinia sniffled again. "Yes. Sometimes he'd appear, and he'd smell like a woman's perfume."

"Like Tommie's perfume?"

Lavinia shrugged. "I can't tell one perfume apart from another, to be honest. Not those cheap perfumes anyway. They all smell alike. And what's more, Tommie's been acting very suspiciously lately."

Both Cressida and I leant forward in our chairs. "What exactly has she done?" Cressida asked her.

Our cakes arrived, once more at an inopportune time. I looked at mine, wondering if I should eat it all now or eat it slowly since two more women were coming to join us, one after the other. When the waitress left, I had forgotten what we were talking about.

So it appeared, had Lavinia. "Didn't you just ask me a question?" She addressed that to Cressida.

Cressida nodded. "I asked what Tommie did that was suspicious."

"Oh yes, she's been sneaking out at all hours of the night. My room is next to hers, as you know, and I've been too afraid to sleep with the murderer on the loose. Every time I hear a noise in the corridor, I peek out, and it's always Tommie."

That didn't sound good to me. "What do you think she's doing?"

Lavinia looked around once more and then spoke in little more than a whisper. "I'm sure Tommie was the one who pushed the tile onto Tristan. I saw her soon after, and she had been acting funny all that day. She comes and goes at strange hours. She's up to no good."

"So if you had to guess whether it was Jemima or Tommie, which one would you say it was?" I asked.

"Possibly Tommie, because she hasn't been working for Peregrine as long, and she would have been upset because he rejected her. You know, that could have been her motive—rejection! Yes, I think it's her."

"What makes you think he rejected her?" I asked.

Lavinia burst into a flood of tears.

I tried to see if they were actual tears or whether she was faking it, but her face was entirely covered with tissues.

Cressida was making soothing sounds. "You poor, poor girl," she said.

After an interval of ensuing silence, Lavinia looked at her phone. "It must be Jemima's turn soon. Thanks for the coffee and cake, and please do not breathe a word of what I've said to Jemima or Tommie. I don't want to be in danger." She grabbed her handbag and hurried away.

Cressida at once turned to me. "Do you think she did it?"

"I have no idea, but I think she was telling the truth about Tommie. We know Tommie was pretending to have a migraine. That at least was a clue. Still, I wanted to ask her if she knew who stood to benefit from the Earl's death."

Two women walked in and looked down their noses at us. A short and loud discussion followed as to where they could possibly sit. Apparently, Cressida and I were occupying their favourite table. They finally moved to sit in front of the fire. Both were dressed in what I always referred to as the *Farmer's Wife Uniform* worn by ex-boarding school women now married to wealthy farmers: high-waisted blue jeans, a blue and white striped shirt with the collar turned up, and a large string of pearls. Both women sported an identical pale blonde bob.

"Do you think they can hear us?" Cressida asked in a stage whisper, drawing scowls from both women.

"Yes," I said in hushed tones. "We had better speak quietly. Hopefully, Jemima won't be drunk at this time of day, and we'll be able to get some sense out of her."

Nanoseconds later, Jemima walked in carrying several bags. "I've been shopping," she said by way of greeting. She sat down where Lavinia had been sitting. "I'll probably have to post them back to myself, because my luggage was just under the limit as it was."

I was pleased her speech wasn't slurring, but my hopes were soon dashed. She looked around her. "We're in a pub. I might get a drink."

"They don't sell drinks in pubs this early in the day in Australia," I told her. "It's illegal."

Her face fell.

"You can have coffee," Cressida offered.

Jemima smiled weakly.

"And go and choose yourself a cake from the display over there." Cressida pointed over her shoulder.

"I don't eat cake," Jemima said. "How else would I keep my figure?"

"Are you enjoying your time here?" Cressida said.

Jemima gasped and then hiccupped. "Of

course not! Peregrine is dead, and I'm staying in a boarding house with the murderer."

"I can assure you that Mr Buttons didn't do it," Cressida said.

Jemima looked as though she was about to argue but thought the better of it.

"Who inherits Peregrine's estate?" I asked her.

Her eyes widened. "He never told me. Besides, he wasn't murdered for his inheritance."

"What makes you think that?" I asked her.

She hesitated. "I don't want to upset you since Mr Buttons is a friend of yours, but he and Peregrine obviously didn't like each other, so I very much doubt Peregrine would have left anything to him."

Cressida's face flushed red. I put a restraining hand on her arm and said, "Let's assume for a moment it wasn't Mr Buttons. Could it have been one of you?"

Jemima frowned deeply. "It's obviously not Tristan because the murderer is after him too."

"Yes, that's puzzling. Why do you think the murderer would want to kill Tristan as well?" I asked her.

"Maybe Tristan is the heir after all," she said.

"Then what reason would Mr Buttons have to kill Tristan?"

She tapped her chin. "You know, I didn't think of that."

"Did Peregrine get on well with both Lavinia and Tommie?"

Jasmine snorted. "He got a little *too* well with Lavinia, if you know what I mean."

I gasped. "Were they in a relationship?"

"Yes, I'm certain of it. I mean, I never caught them in the act or anything like that, but they often touched hands when they thought nobody was looking, and they certainly acted as though something was going on."

Cressida frowned deeply. "Why were they surreptitious? They weren't married to other people, so why did they have to keep it a secret?"

At this point, the waitress returned and did a double-take to see a different woman sitting with us. "Coffee?" she asked Jemima.

"A long black," Jemima said. "No cake." She watched the waitress leave and added, "I have no idea. I assumed it was because Peregrine had another woman on the side. He was a terrible flirt. He used to flirt with me, and I had to put him in his place. In fact, it was quite hard to work for him at first, but he lost interest after a while, so I assumed he was seeing someone else."

"Could it have been Tommie?" I asked her.

"Tommie? I don't know. She hadn't been working for him for long. Maybe it was her, but I'm sure he had plenty of other women in his social circle."

"Was Lavinia ever upset that he didn't make their relationship public?" I asked her.

"Who knows? You would have to ask her. Do you suspect Lavinia?"

Cressida and I exchanged glances. "We know it wasn't Mr Buttons," I told her. "That means it has to be one of you."

She did not appear offended in the least. "That's a scary thought. I've been assuming it was Mr Buttons." She trembled a little. "Well, if it wasn't Mr Buttons, then it could have been Tommie. She's been acting suspiciously lately, creeping around, coming and going at strange hours. She's definitely hiding something."

Jemima stood up. "I don't want coffee after all. Is that all right? I need to go and buy some wine. Surely I can buy it somewhere?" Without another word, she hurried out the door.

"See, I told you it was a good idea to question

these girls," Cressida said. "We've discovered that Tommie's been acting strangely."

"And you think I murdered Peregrine?" came an upset voice behind us.

We swung around. Tommie was standing there.

CHAPTER 16

"I didn't see you there," Cressida said.

"Obviously."

Tommie stalked in and threw herself onto the seat Jemima had just vacated. "I saw Jemima go, so I thought I'd come early. I'm in a hurry. I have somewhere else to be."

"Look, we mean no offence, Tommie," I said, "but to be perfectly honest, we asked you all here to question you, because we know Mr Buttons is not the murderer."

"Well, it's not me." Tommie folded her arms over her chest. "What motive would I possibly have?"

"Were you in a relationship with him?"

Tommie appeared puzzled. "With whom?"

"The Earl," I said, stating the obvious.

Tommie pulled a face. "Eww! Certainly not! He's not my type." She shuddered.

"There have been reports that you've been coming and going at odd hours and acting secretively."

Tommie leant forward and put her face in her hands. "I knew it was going to come out sometime. I mean, I do have to go back to England presently."

"What are you talking about?" I prompted in the gentlest tones I could muster.

"The horse, of course!"

"The horse?" Cressida and I exclaimed in unison.

"Yes, I stole the horse."

"The blue horse?" I asked her.

She nodded and pulled some cash out of her handbag. She slid it across the table to me. "I'm terribly sorry, Sibyl, but I stole your products. Please don't tell the police."

Cressida folded her arms over her chest. "Let me get this straight. Am I to understand you broke into Sibyl's van, stole her expensive products, and drained my tank, simply to turn a horse blue?"

Tommie ignored Cressida and spoke to me. "I'm terribly sorry that I stole your products, but that money will cover it, won't it?"

I looked down at the notes. "Yes, that's about what it cost me. Tommie, whatever possessed you to do such a thing?"

"When we were first driving from Little Tatterford to the boarding house with Peregrine, we took a wrong turn and ended up down a laneway. I saw a very thin horse. She was shockingly thin, so I insisted that we stop. I got out and spoke to the owner. He said he was a horse dealer, that he buys one or two at a time and sells them for more money."

"Then maybe he was going to fatten up the poor horse," Cressida said.

She shook her head vigorously. "No! He said he'd already had the horse for two months. Two months! Can you believe it? The horse was very thin. I asked if I could buy her, but I had already got him offside by then, so he called me some very rude words and ordered me to get off his property. Later that night, I went back and stole the horse. I put her in that paddock behind your house, Cressida. I bought some hay to feed her."

"But didn't you think you'd get caught eventually?" I asked her.

She threw up her hands, palms upwards, to the ceiling. "Honestly, I just had to act. That poor horse."

I thought about it. "Hmm, Blake said the stolen horse was a pale palomino. I suppose she was covered with red dirt and was a cream colour like a pale palomino due to years of not being washed."

Tommie readily agreed. "That's why I wanted to turn her back to grey. The awful man referred to her as a washed-out palomino, so I knew nobody would be looking for a grey horse."

"So that's why you've been sneaking around all the time?" I asked her.

"Yes, it's been extremely stressful," she said with a sigh. "Thankfully, I've had some help."

I suspected I knew who that was. "You mean the lady at the produce store in town?"

Tommie nodded slowly. "Yes, such a nice lady. She sold me that rug very cheaply for the horse and sold me some lucerne hay cheaply too. She knows about that man, the one I stole the horse from. She says he's horrible. The only thing is, I'm going back to England, and I don't know what to do with the horse."

"Sibyl, you're buying that land from me, aren't you?"

I turned to Cressida. "Yes, why?"

"We can put the horse on your land when Tommie goes back to England."

"A stolen horse on my land?" I said in horror. "Cressida, haven't you forgotten that my boyfriend is a police officer?"

"Then why don't you offer to buy the mare from the nasty man? That would make it all legal."

Before I could answer, Tommie said, "She's an old horse. You wouldn't be able to ride her."

I thought about the whole situation. "No, that's fine. I'll go and see the man and make sure he sells her to me."

"What if he refuses?" Tommie said. "He'll suspect you have the horse, and he'll come and get her."

"You leave that to me," I said. "He's a dealer. He would have sold her to you if he hadn't been angry with you. I think I can handle him."

Tommie grabbed my hand. A tear trickled down her cheek. It was a genuine tear, unlike

Lavinia's—or so I suspected. Maybe Lavinia's tears were genuine, after all.

"Thank you, Sibyl. I can't thank you enough. I've worried myself sick about that horse."

"And now perhaps you can return the favour," Cressida said. "We know for a fact Mr Buttons didn't kill the Earl. That only leaves one of you."

"The murderer was after Tristan too," Tommie said. "As it isn't Tristan, it must be Lavinia or Jemima."

"Who do you think it is?" I asked her.

"I don't know. I haven't had much of a chance to think about it, what with the horse and everything. I'm certain Lavinia was in a relationship with Peregrine. Lavinia didn't seem to like me, and I'm sure she thought I was secretly in a relationship with the Earl too. I also wondered if Jemima was as well."

"Did you ever see him in public with a woman?" I asked her.

She shook her head. "The other three have been working for him for ages, but I only started working for him recently," she said. "My brother played polo with the Earl, so that's how I got the job. We're a horsey family, you see. I do Three Day Eventing."

I was about to ask her something else, but she was still speaking. "And I'm afraid I lied to earlier. You see, I wasn't supposed to know."

"What do you mean?"

Tommie fidgeted. "You asked me if I knew who inherits the Earl's estate."

"And you said you didn't. Were you lying? Do you know?"

"Yes, I do. I wasn't supposed to know," she repeated, "and that's why I didn't tell you, but when I was sneaking around, I overheard Tristan on the phone with his lawyer. Tristan inherits everything."

CHAPTER 17

Cressida and I were at a loss. As I watched Tommie's departing back, I said, "Surely the detectives know that Tristan stands to gain from the Earl's death?"

"But if they do know, then why isn't Tristan the prime suspect?" Cressida asked. "We need to confront him."

"No way! If he's the murderer, we would be in terrible danger."

"Then what are we going to do?"

I thought about it for a moment. "I'll tell Blake. I'll say we were having coffee with Tommie when she let slip that Tristan is the Earl's heir."

Cressida appeared relieved. "What a good

idea. Shall we go home now? I don't think it's safe for us to stay at the boarding house. Mr Buttons and I will need to stay in your house again tonight, Sibyl."

I did my best not to grimace. "First of all, let's go to the nearest ATM, and then I'm going to speak to that horse dealer."

I was surprised Cressida didn't ask a million questions, and before long we were driving to the horse dealer's little farm. The directions Tommie had given were clear.

"I didn't realise he lived down this road and so close to my home," Cressida said. "What are you going to say to him, Sibyl?"

"You stay here," I said. "He might feel threatened if he sees two people. He's obviously a cowardly type. I'll go alone."

"If you're sure, Sibyl." Cressida pursed her lips. "If you get into trouble, run for the car. I'll keep the engine running, and we can make a quick getaway."

I chuckled. "He's not the murderer, Cressida. I'm sure I'll be fine."

I made my way to the man's house. I didn't see any animals, much to my relief. He certainly didn't sound like somebody who should be responsible for animals. The property was unkempt, and the fences were in poor condition. Some of them were leaning over, but I noticed strands of white electric tape running inside the fences. I made a mental note not to touch anything.

I walked around to the back of the house, intending to walk to the back door, when I spotted him over by a tall woodpile. He looked up at me, a wood splitter in his hand and a suspicious expression on his face. "What do you want?"

"I want to buy a horse," I said. I pulled out a wad of cash and flipped through it in front of him.

His eyes widened. He almost drooled. "I don't have a horse," he snapped. "I had a horse, but she's missing."

"I heard about that," I said. "Palomino, wasn't she?"

He nodded. "A pale one but I'm sure if you fed her up well, she'd go a nice deep golden colour in summer."

I very much doubted that, given she was grey. Still, I refrained from commenting. Instead I said, "How much do you want for her?"

"How much have you got?"

I handed him the cash. "This is all I've got, and I don't have a cent more."

He stared fixedly at the money. "The only thing is, she's not here. I reported her to the cops, but they haven't found her yet." He held up both hands, palms upwards. "How can a horse disappear? It's ridiculous. It's not as if Captain Thunderbolt is still around in this century, holding up stagecoaches, robbing people, stealing horses, and all that."

"I did hear a neighbour had found a pale palomino horse," I said. "I liked the look of her, so I asked around who owned her and they told me to come and see you."

"Where is she?"

"Um, she was out on the road so they put her in a paddock." I stuck out my hand. "Do we have a deal?"

He shook my hand.

"You need to sign a bill of sale to make it legal and all that," I said. "My boyfriend is a cop, and he's very particular about such things."

All the colour drained from the man's face. "Um, um, a cop?" he sputtered.

I pulled a piece of paper out of my pocket. I had hastily written on the back of a napkin at the

Top Pub. "Sign and date here," I said, "and then you can keep all that money."

The man couldn't sign fast enough. "You have to agree never to buy another horse. I believe you've had that mare for a long time, and she's quite thin."

He took a step forward, his manner menacing. "Now look here, girly…"

I put my hands on my hips. "Do you want me to call my boyfriend?"

He hesitated. "What's his name?"

"Sergeant Wessley."

He narrowed his eyes and took another look at me. "You live up at the boarding house, don't you?"

Technically, I lived in the cottage on the boarding house grounds, but I simply said, "Yes."

"There was a murder there the other day." He said it as though it was an accusation.

"Yes, that's right," I said.

"They've been a few murders there, haven't there!"

I continued to nod. "Yes, several murders. They were all done by different people, nobody at the boarding house."

He jutted out his chin in a belligerent manner. "Says you."

I winked at him. "Only somebody very clever and ruthless could pin all those murders at the boarding house on other people. So, do we have a deal? You will agree never to buy a horse again?"

He backed away. "Sure, sure, whatever you want."

I waved my index finger at him. "I'll be keeping my eye on you."

The man turned and ran inside his house. I walked back to the car, waving the contract at Cressida.

She broke into a wide grin.

"Congratulations, Sibyl. You now own a horse."

"Tommie will be pleased. Cressida, could you drop me back at my cottage? I want to go through some paperwork for my upcoming appointments."

Five minutes later, I walked inside my cottage. Max was perched on the back of a chair. He greeted me with his usual string of obscenities. I shooed him out of the window.

Sandy was excited to see me because, being a typical Labrador, she thought the appearance of a human meant she would get a treat. I gave her a treat and then sat at the little desk in the corner and called Blake. It went straight to voicemail, so I left a message to tell him Tristan was the Earl's heir.

I was waiting for my laptop to boot up when there was a knock on the door. I assumed Cressida had forgotten something or wanted to strong-arm me into having a cup of tea with her.

I opened the door. To my horror, Tristan was standing there.

"Are you all right, Sibyl? You look as though you've seen a ghost."

"Yes, I'm all right," I said rather too brightly. "What can I do for you?"

"Aren't you going to invite me in?"

He was already halfway through the door. I figured if I slammed it in his face, he could bust it open. I decided it was better to play along as though nothing was wrong. "Sure, come in," I said.

"Mr Buttons was quite upset when he came back."

"Does he think they will arrest him?" I asked in alarm.

Tristan shrugged. "Sibyl, there's something I

need to tell you, and I'm sorry I didn't tell you before."

"What is it?" I asked him.

He sat down on the couch. "I'm the heir."

I feigned surprise. "You're the heir?"

"I didn't want to admit to being the heir because I thought everybody would suspect me."

"Have you told the police?" I asked him.

"Yes, of course."

"So why don't they suspect you?"

He shrugged. "Maybe they do?"

I thought about it. "There was an attempt on your life. Who would benefit from your death?"

Tristan stood up and paced up and down the small room. "That's what I don't understand. I haven't even made a will yet. I know I should, but I haven't bothered, to be honest. I don't have a girlfriend or a wife or children. I don't know who would get anything if something were to happen to me, and I don't have much of anything to pass on."

"But you do now, once the Earl's estate is settled," I pointed out.

He drew his hand over his forehead. "I'm certainly not leaving anything to Tommie, Lavinia, or Jemima, so I don't understand why an attempt was made on my life. That's what I wanted to discuss with you."

He gestured to the couch and sat down. I sat beside him, as far away as I could.

"Sibyl, I don't want to offend you, but I think Mr Buttons did it."

"Why would Mr Buttons want to murder you?"

"I have no idea, to be honest."

"Tristan, Mr Buttons didn't do it, I can assure you. Do you really think he's the murderer?"

Tristan sighed. "If it wasn't him, then I have to face the fact it was one of my friends."

"If it was one of them, which one would you suspect?"

He rubbed his eyes. "I think Tommie or Lavinia did it. I've given it a lot of thought, and that's all I can come up with. I've told the detectives my concerns, but I don't know whether they listened to me."

He hesitated, and I waved one hand at him. "Please go on."

"Lavinia was having an affair with Peregrine."

"Do you know that for a fact, or is that simply a suspicion?"

Tristan nodded vigorously. "It's a fact.

Peregrine always told me all about his affairs. He said he'd been having an affair with her for years, and she was insanely jealous of other women."

I shook my head. "Why do you call it an affair? Neither of them were married to other people," I said. "Did he have a regular girlfriend?"

It was Tristan's turn to shake his head. "I suppose I called it an affair because it was all so horribly furtive, the two of them sneaking about. He was also sneaking about with Tommie. And I think maybe Lavinia tried to kill me because I discouraged Peregrine from his relationship with her. I didn't expect he would tell her, but maybe he did."

"That would explain why she wanted to kill you, but why would she want to kill the Earl?"

Tristan appeared exasperated. "Peregrine was the most terrible flirt," he said. "Lavinia wanted something more. This has been going on for years, and I think she finally snapped."

"So you think it was Lavinia and not Tommie?"

"That's what I thought, but Tommie's been acting very strangely lately."

"I discovered what that was about," I said. I told him all about the horse. "So Cressida and I have just been to see the horse dealer, and I bought the horse from him," I concluded. "So the whole thing about Tommie sneaking around was all due to the horse."

Tristan looked doubtful. "That doesn't discount the fact that she could have murdered Peregrine. Tommie was seeing him as well. I told the police that. I was worried Lavinia might try to kill Tommie, or Tommie might try to do away with Lavinia. They were both romantically involved with Peregrine, you see, and I was actively trying to discourage him from dating either of them. My advice to him was that as he couldn't choose between them, then he should get rid of them both and try to find himself a decent woman."

My head was spinning. "Do you think the Earl told both women your opinion?"

He shrugged. "Why else would somebody try to drop a tile on my head? You know, it was probably Tommie. She drained the tank at the back of the house when she washed the horse, right? Maybe she saw those tiles in the tool shed, as it's next to the tank she drained. She tried to drop one of those tiles on my head to get me out of the picture."

I bit one fingernail as a cold shiver ran up my spine. I thought over his words for a moment. "So you don't suspect Jemima at all?" I asked him.

Tristan's mouth formed a perfect O. "Jemima? No. She's always drunk. I doubt anyone so inebriated would be able drop a tile from the roof. Besides, she wasn't having an affair with Peregrine. He would have told me."

"You know, Jemima was the one who told Mr Buttons that the Earl wanted tequila." I shut my eyes and tried to recall the events.

"Any one of us could have done that," Tristan said dismissively.

"And Jemima was the one who got us all to walk away from Peregrine and look at Cressida's painting on the wall. That action gave the murderer the opportunity to slip the poison into the Earl's tequila."

"I do take your point," Tristan said, smiling and nodding, "but if she was engaging everyone in conversation over that horrendous painting—no offence intended—then how did she slip the poison into the Earl's tequila?"

I thought about it some more, and that's when I knew beyond a shadow of a doubt who had murdered Peregrine Winthrop-Montgomery-Rose-Bucklefort, the Fifth Earl of Mockingbird.

CHAPTER 18

I did my best to keep a neutral expression on my face. "Did you tell the detectives you suspect Lavinia and Tommie?" I asked him.

"Yes, I did," Tristan said.

I nodded and tried to keep my tone casual. "Cressida has invited me up to the boarding house for a cup of tea. Let's walk there. I want to check on Mr Buttons."

I made for the door, but Tristan barred my way. "You noticed my slip up, didn't you?"

"Slip up?" I repeated. "What slip up was that?"

"You're not a very good liar, Sibyl," Tristan said. His cold tone sent further shivers up my spine. “I saw your face when I said it. I kept chatting on, hoping you hadn’t noticed, but when you asked about Jemima, I realised the gig was up.”

I opened my mouth to protest, but he forestalled me. “I know you’re onto us.”

What was I going to do? Blake was at work. Cressida and Mr Buttons were in the boarding house. I was alone in my cottage with Tristan.

Tristan opened the door a crack and peeked out. As quick as a flash, I pulled the phone from my jeans pocket and swiped it to open. I pressed redial and popped it back in my pocket, right in the nick of time.

As Tristan turned around, I pulled a tissue from my pocket and pretended to sniffle into it.

I backed away. “How would you have known that the bathroom tiles were in the tool shed? Only the person who dropped the tile off the roof would know that. Since you couldn’t possibly have been the person who dropped it off the roof, that meant you had an accomplice.”

“I realised you had put two and two together when you asked about Jemima,” he said.

“So you and Jemima murdered the Earl?” I asked him. “Why?”

He shrugged. "Isn't it obvious? I inherit everything. I tolerated that awful man for years. I knew if I waited long enough, the police wouldn't suspect me of his murder, because I've been his driver for more than ten years now. I'm his only living relative."

That surprised me. "I didn't know you were a relative!"

"Yes, we're cousins. I told the police all this."

"Why did you try to pin it on Mr Buttons?" I asked him.

"He was the perfect person to take the fall," Tristan said rather smugly. "Mr Buttons and Peregrine go way back, and their relationship was acrimonious. Of course, the detectives suspected Mr Buttons. That was my intent. I cooperated with them and helped them along that train of thought."

"And you're giving a cut to Jemima," I guessed.

"Yes, a rather sizeable cut, more's the pity. I needed her help to distract everybody when I poisoned Peregrine, and I needed somebody to push that tile off the roof. I knew that would throw the detectives off my scent. Mind you, her aim was off. It was a little *too* close."

"I take it Jemima isn't quite the drunk she makes out?"

"That's right."

I remembered the ute. "Was that a coincidence, or was that Jemima in the ute that ran us off the road?"

"Yes, that was absolutely spiffing! She stole the vehicle from a nearby farmer and returned it. I doubt the farmer ever knew it was missing. It was unlocked, and she hot-wired it. Miss-spent youth and all that."

"The locals never lock their cars. And you were the one who put the poison in the Earl's drink?"

Tristan smirked. "Yes, I did it."

"How did you manage to get so much methanol into his glass?" I asked him.

"Good grief, I didn't slip too much into his glass. I'd been poisoning him for some time." He waved one hand at me in dismissal.

"But weren't you worried the authorities would discover that in the autopsy?" I asked him.

Tristan's face registered shock. "Of course not. That's why I murdered him in Australia. I'm sure your police procedural people here are quite backwards, like the rest of you. I knew I'd get away with it. And now..."

His voice trailed away as he took a step towards me, his hands outstretched.

I ducked away from him and fell backwards over Sandy, who was sleeping through the whole thing. As I scrambled away, I heard wings.

I only paused when Tristan screamed. I looked up. Max was sitting on Tristan's head. "Spin, Bobbits, spin, you &%-^$^!" he squawked.

It took me a moment to realise Tristan did indeed look like Detective Roberts. My cockatoo had apparently mistaken Tristan for the detective. And it appeared my cockatoo held a grudge.

Tristan screamed louder as Max's claws dug deeper. The door flung open. Blake burst inside, a uniformed officer close behind him. Blake seized Tristan and threw him to the floor. He landed with a loud thud.

Max squawked some further insults before moving out of the way. Blake handcuffed Tristan, and the uniformed officer bundled him out of my cottage. Blake hurried over to me and helped me up. "Are you all right?"

I shook my head. I was on the verge of tears. "He and Jemima were in it together," I told him.

Blake stroked my hair. "Yes, we heard everything. Thank goodness you managed to turn your phone on. We heard everything," he repeated.

"Tristan just turned up here," I said. "I didn't want to invite him in, but I thought it would look suspicious if I didn't. I wasn't certain he was the murderer at that stage."

"It's all right, don't worry about it," Blake said.

I looked out of the open door to see Max pecking at the window of the police vehicle.

CHAPTER 19

I had fallen asleep on the couch watching TV, and I awoke with a burning sensation prickling my face. I trudged into my bathroom, leaving a trail of chocolate wrappers, and caught sight of the Swamp Thing in the mirror. Only it wasn't the Swamp Thing.

"I need to cancel," I told Blake the second he picked up the phone. I was still in the bathroom, panicking.

"We're not cancelling," Blake said.

"But, but," I stammered. "I've fallen into a vat of radioactive waste. I can't go to the restaurant."

"Sibyl! I'll be there in ten."

I hung up the phone and sniffled. How on earth had this happened? I was very careful with my skin. Sometimes I even drank water instead of wine. Sometimes. Not often, but the effort was there.

I went back to the couch. There were pine cones everywhere. That could mean only one thing. "Sandy!" I called out, and the naughty dog padded into the room. "I told you not to bring pine cones into the house."

Sandy woofed happily.

"No," I said. "Bad dog."

Sandy wagged her tail and woofed again.

"It's no use," I grumbled to myself, handing her a treat.

If Blake didn't accept me at my Swamp Thing, then he did not deserve me at my best. Still, when I heard his car outside, I ducked into the bathroom again and slathered a cucumber mask all over my face.

When Blake caught sight of me, he gasped and said, "Oh!" He cleared his throat. "You look nice."

"The pine cones attacked me."

He chuckled. "Where are they? I'll show them no one messes with my girlfriend."

"Sandy tore up pine cones in my couch. I

must have been too tired to notice, and I fell asleep."

"At least you smell good," Blake replied. "Like Christmas."

"Can we do this dinner another time?"

"Absolutely not. Take off that face mask. If you don't want to go to the restaurant, we'll have dinner here."

I hurried back to the bathroom. I ran a cloth under warm water and used it to wipe my skin clear.

When I walked back into the living room, Blake said, "On second thoughts, put it back on."

"Ha ha," I said. "Very funny."

"I'll get you an antihistamine. Sit on the couch and put your feet up. You don't need to worry about a thing. I'll make you dinner."

"You mean you'll order pizza."

"Isn't that the same thing as making dinner?"

"I believe so."

"That's why we're so compatible." Blake bopped me on the nose before I could swat away his hand.

The antihistamine worked rapidly. I figured I still looked like a monster, but at least I didn't want to scratch my face into oblivion. Honestly, I had turned up looking a lot worse on dates.

"Are you having a reaction?" Blake called. He was putting pizza on my grandmother's finest china.

"I'm okay," I said.

We decided to eat in front of the television. I made Blake watch *The Bachelor*, which he pretended to hate, but I heard him gasp during the rose ceremony. "I can't believe she didn't get a rose," he muttered. "I'll bet the producers told him not to send that mean one home."

I couldn't speak as I'd just taken a large bite of pizza.

"What a terrible show," Blake said when I turned off the television. "What day is it on next?"

I swallowed my pizza and laughed. It felt as though my rash had gone down a little, but I didn't want to check. I decided to pretend I had the skin of an angel instead and get on with my evening, which would have been much easier to do if Cressida hadn't burst into my cottage.

"Why didn't you knock?" I said, surprised.

Cressida sighed. "I don't have the time for your boring rules, Sibyl. I'm on a mission."

"What's wrong?"

"Nothing's wrong," she replied, "only the ice sculpture was accidently delivered to my place, and the delivery man insists Blake sign for it."

"Ice sculpture?" I said. "What ice sculpture?"

Blake's face flushed bright red. "Er, yes. Come on then, Cressida. I'll sign for the delivery man. Sibyl, you stay here."

"Is it a surprise for me?" I asked hopefully. "Is that why I can't see the ice sculpture?

"I just don't want you to scare the man," Blake said. Luckily for him, he dodged my swat.

"You smell like Christmas." Cressida smiled at me as she followed Blake out of the cottage.

I threw myself down onto the couch. Sandy came over and licked my hand, which was her way of apologising for the pine cones, or so I liked to think.

I was drifting off to sleep again when I heard my name. "Sibyl?"

Blake stuck his head around the front door. "Would you come outside?"

"Is Cressida outside?" I asked.

"No," he replied, "just the ice sculpture. Come on."

I took a deep breath and grabbed Blake's

hand. He led me outside to the paddock next to the cottage. There, sparkling in the moonlight, was a beautiful ice sculpture. I squinted, not sure what I was seeing at first, and then I saw the ice was carved into a swan.

I threw myself into Blake's arms and kissed him. He kissed me back. Then he put me down, and he raked a hand through his hair, blushing.

"This is amazing," I squealed.

"Thank you," he replied. "It's easy being wonderful to you."

I was about to kiss him again when I heard the sound of someone chipping ice. I swung around.

"Oh, please don't mind me," Mr Buttons said. "I was rather in the mood for a drink, and there is no ice left at Cressida's. Or in the Southern Hemisphere I should think."

"Do you mind?" Blake said. "We're in the middle of something."

"I'm in the middle of something too," Mr Buttons replied. "A drink. I wouldn't mind a spot of television. Is anything good on tonight? We can all watch TV, or we could reminisce about solving the murder."

Blake and I looked at each other.

Mr Buttons raised his glass. "I'll wait for you in the cottage. Cressida will be along presently."

"I'm here now!" Cressida appeared out of the night, silhouetted by the rising moon, and looking for all the world like an apparition, albeit an apparition clutching a large hamper. "Albert sent this along for us. I have champagne—proper French champagne!—and roasted red pepper tapenade, pesto baguette sandwiches, cheese gougeres, and other words I can't pronounce. We can have a post-murder-solving party in your cottage, Sibyl."

"Isn't it wonderful to have friends!" Mr Buttons said. "I would probably be under arrest now if it wasn't for all of you. I was facing dark times, dark times indeed, but now I have come out on the other side, and all is well."

Cressida nodded so vigorously that her false eyelashes fell off. Sandy promptly ate them. "Yes, that's the way of it, Mr Buttons," she said. "It's like a rainbow. Dark times never last, even if it seems as though they will at the time. We all face storms in our lives, but once we're through the storms, we come out to be greeted by sunshine and rainbows."

Cressida and Mr Buttons linked arms and

walked inside, followed by Sandy who was looking hopefully up at Cressida's face.

As soon as they disappeared, I kissed Blake. "How did you get so perfect?"

"It's a burden," he sighed. "Are you okay? You look a little flushed."

"I feel a little hot." I picked up one of Mr Buttons' discarded ice chips and pressed it against my forehead, not even wincing when it melted and ran down my face. Actually, it helped to cool the itchy skin caused by the pine cones.

After a moment or two, Blake looked deep into my eyes. "Are you okay?"

I did feel a little faint. After all, only hours earlier a murderer had been intent upon doing away with me. I leant into Blake as though I was going to topple over.

"Don't fall," he said.

"Oh," I replied, "I fell a long time ago."

"Well," Blake said, "that's another thing we have in common."

ABOUT MORGANA BEST

USA Today bestselling author Morgana Best survived a childhood of deadly spiders and venomous snakes in the Australian outback. Morgana Best writes cozy mysteries and enjoys thinking of delightful new ways to murder her victims.

www.morganabest.com